THE CARRIER

Tell-Tale Publishing's 9th Annual Horror Anthology

TT
www.tell-talepublishing.com

NIGHTSHADE

TABLE OF CONTENTS

THE CARRIER

Shawn D. Brink

The carrier arrived in Earth's orbit. Moments later, a swarm of single-passenger shuttle pods released from its docking bays. Anne's pod auto-piloted to its programed landing spot in sector 127 without incident.

She safely checked the seals of her biohazard suit. Then, once the pod's onboard computer indicated that the outer hull had sufficiently cooled, she opened the exit hatch, climbed out, and stood for the first time on the planet of her ancestors.

It wasn't COVID-19 that ended human life on Earth, but the far deadlier COVID-34. Wearing masks did nothing to stop this variant either. Social distancing didn't even slow it down. There was no time to develop a vaccine and there was no way to effectively quarantine.

All known humans now live on Mars. It'd been three decades since the colonists first arrived on the Red Planet. Now, a population boom pushed its resources to the limit, necessitating a mission back to Earth to explore the possibility of recolonization.

Anne pulled up her map file of sector 127, and it promptly displayed on a transparent screen in the upper-right corner of her helmet's visor. The map's headline indicated that sector 127 had once been called the Badlands of South Dakota, in a country once known as the United States.

She used the map to locate highway 240, or what was left of it. The highway wasn't more than crumbling asphalt with thick patches of prairie grass crowding its many cracks. Still, it looked sufficient for hover-scoot navigation.

She removed her backpack, opened it, and pulled out the hover-scoot components. She hooked up the battery, assembled the handlebars and support rod, and then connected it all to the footboard.

Her backpack felt lighter now as she hover-scooted north, navigating around rusted-out vehicles dotting the highway. Through the grimy windows of some of these, she spied the mummified silhouettes of those entombed within.

Such macabre dioramas didn't surprise Anne. History classes taught about COVID-34, and how it moved so fast that the distance from healthy to dead was crossed in seconds.

2034 was a big year for humankind. Not only was it the year of its extinction on Earth but was also when a rocket emblazoned with the words "Mars or Bust" blasted off, filled with the first ever interplanetary colonists. Those colonists had no way of knowing then how perfect their timing was, disembarking just days before the COVID-34 mutation occurrence.

Within two weeks after blasting off, Earth-to-ship transmissions ceased. Recorded news briefs were still received however, all of them telling doomsday scenarios.

Now, as Anne hovered along 240, she wondered if every human actually died in the pandemic. She hoped so. If everyone died, then the virus would have had no one to infect. If the virus had no one to infect, it would have also died out. And if the virus was dead, then Earth could safely be re-populated.

She stopped the hover-scoot. A corroded sign on an angled pole indicated she was entering Wall, South Dakota – the only town of any size in sector 127, and where she assumed humans would be found, if any existed.

Movement! She unholstered her Gen12 Glock and zeroed in on the target.

Some twenty yards away, a skin-and-bones dog sat in the dust, lethargically scratching its ear with its hind leg. It was a short-haired, medium-sized breed that Anne didn't recognize – probably the result of multi-generation-mutt-breeding without human intervention.

She kept the Glock's laser-site on it for a few minutes, but the feral mutt acted neither fearful nor aggressive. Satisfied the dog was no threat, Anne re-holstered her weapon and pulled up the map file once more.

Highway 240 was called Glenn Street once it entered Wall. She cruised along Glenn, calling out through her suit's built-in megaphone: "Hello. I come in peace. Is anyone here? Please respond. Let me know you are here."

Most of the town's buildings were in advanced states of decay – little more than piles of rubble. Here and there, she saw what looked like sun-bleached bones, shining in the sun like old elephant tusks.

She took a left at the corner of Glenn and 6th Avenue, and there was that dog again. It trotted along, keeping pace with Anne, its tongue dangling and flopping with the bounce of its gait. Anne kept a wary eye, resting her palm on the handle of her holstered Glock as it loped along.

It stopped, lifted a hind leg, and peed on a mostly brown shrub. Then, it disappeared around the rotting remains of a partially collapsed building.

She took 6th Avenue to Main and then turned right. Here was a big building, one that still stood upright for the most part. The green and yellow sign above the entrance was weathered and loose, but still legible – *Wall Drug Store, Since 1931.*

Anne dismounted the hover-scoot and entered Wall Drug. "Hello, is anyone here?" she repeatedly called out as she explored the dilapidated building.

There were more bones in here. They were dry, old-looking bones. Whatever flesh had once been on them, had long since turned to dust.

She searched the entire building but found no signs of human habitation. Satisfied her sector was safe, she radioed in the "all clear". A few seconds later, her transmission was acknowledged with a recorded message stating that a transport of colonists were being automatically deployed from the carrier above – estimated arrival time: 40 minutes.

She sat down in the ruins of Wall Drug, resting her back against an old sign that advertised cups of coffee for a nickel. With her mission complete, fatigue engulfed her. She closed her eyes and rested.

***

Something startled Anne awake – a noise. She turned toward it and unholstered her Glock in one fluid motion.

It was the dog, but it no longer appeared indifferent to her presence. Its hackles bristled. Its teeth showed. A malicious growl came from deep inside.

She centered the red dot of her weapon's laser site between its eyes.

A second dog emerged from around the corner, exposing its sharp teeth, its loose coat of mangy hair vibrating with the low growl emanating from its throat.

"Good boys," she squeaked through her suit's speaker. "Be good boys."

A third dog appeared, then a fourth. The pack growled in unison, tightening the circle around her.

She shifted her aim from one dog to the next, but didn't pull the trigger. Killing them would be a last resort. She couldn't off them all at once and didn't know if firing her gun would spook them away or entice an attack.

A fifth dog jumped her from behind, ripping her helmet's clear-vinyl face shield to shreds with its large teeth. She held it back, its iron jaws snapping inches from her face. Flecks of spittle hit her skin. Its breath was horrid.

A second dog went for her jugular but got her suit's thick collar instead. She pressed the Glock point-blank against its chest and pulled the trigger.

The flash and boom created disorientation. For a moment, everything stilled. Then, the dogs jumped back. She pulled the trigger again.

Yipping, the remainders fled. She pushed the lifeless carcass away and staggered to her feet.

Blood and hair coated her. The smell was sickening.

She wiped saliva from her exposed face and tried to call in an update, but her radio wasn't operational. The wiring had been damaged in the melee.

Anne made her way outside of Wall Drug. She needed to warn the soon-to-arrive colonists about this danger. She stared into the sky and saw what looked like a falling star – *the landing transport.*

She began to cough, lightly at first. Within a minute though, they became full-body spasms. Vertigo followed.

Realization hit her like a bag of bricks. *The dogs are COVID carriers!*

But this wasn't COVID-19, or even COVID-34. This was a new variant, a canine-asymptomatic variant.

Anne took two more steps before collapsing in the dust. She heard growling and looked up. An army of dogs emerged from various hidey-holes, surrounding her – tightening the circle.

Then, another sound – the roar of landing thrusters.

She tried to warn the ship, but her shouts were only wheezes. They'd never hear her anyway, not with the sound of those thrusters firing. No one on that ship would know about the dogs until the hatch opened. And then, it could be too late.

The thrusters powered down as the ship landed. She aimed the Glock at its hull and fired her weapon until it was empty. Her shots wouldn't damage the ship, but they would register on its computer. It was the only warning she could think to provide.

The ground shook as the transport lifted off. The dogs moved in.

Anne's bones were added to their collection.

MYSTICAL BEATS

Elizabeth Alsobrooks

Mai refused to wipe a hand across her bleeding mouth as she rose, feet not as steady as her ramrod posture suggested. She cursed; an inward threat directed outward toward the man her Mamaw insisted they must endure for now. Then she inhaled, deeply. She tried to pull it back, the rage she directed at him, because she felt something, something dangerous that wrapped itself around his neck and began to squeeze.

His own feet unsteady, the thin, bearded, self-proclaimed Cajun shoved a hand to grab the edge of the kitchen sink. His bloodshot blue eyes studied it for a moment, as if deciding whether to hurl or keep yelling. Deciding on the latter, he glared over at Mai and snarled, "Where yer Mamaw be? Ain't no dinner here neither."

She sighed, her irritation under control again. All she'd done was accidentally walk out of the kitchen as he walked in and bumped into him. He immediately backhanded her out of his way. How much longer must she tolerate this man? Did Mamaw even love him? Mai didn't believe it. She walked to the refrigerator and pulled out the large heavy pot Mamaw prepared before she left for work. "She had a later shift today, but she made some of her gumbo. I'll heat it up."

Thankfully satisfied, he stumbled forward and reached past her to grab a beer, gestured to her mouth and muttered, "Sorry 'bout dat. Rough day," and headed for the living room to watch TV and do what he did best, drink. How he held down that job at the docks she'd never know, but it paid well, all things considered. Mamaw depended on him to pay the rent on a much nicer house in a much nicer neighborhood than they could have afforded on their own. More surprising was that for some reason he gave Mamaw money for groceries and gave her the occasional trinket too. *During his rare sober moments, he probably realizes she's way out of his league,* Mai mused.

Mai swiped a half towel off the roll and dampened it. She held it to her split lip as she clicked the stove knob to flame the rich Creole dish made often as Renard loved it, so it helped keep him in a congenial mood.

She turned her head as the kitchen door opened and Mamaw sailed in. "Oh, good, you've got the pot on. Guess what I brought home?"

Renard strolled into the kitchen, and she turned to him, proudly holding up a large loaf of French bread that smelled heavenly fresh. "That new cook, Genny, snuck this into my hand as I was leaving today. Just baked!"

"Hey, dat smell good," Renard drawled.

Taking in her husband's condition at a glance, she said, "Sit down. Let me cut this and you can start in on that until the gumbo's done. You must be starving."

"Could eat a horse, cher, but yer gumbo sure hit da spot."

The way to this man's heart went straight through his stomach for sure, Mai thought. Not wanting Mamaw to see her lip, she said, "I'm gonna be late for work. I've gotta go."

"Well take this at least," her Mamaw said, shoving a chunk of bread into her hand.

She held it up to her mouth, hiding her split lip and said, "Thanks. See you later."

***

"Shit! What the fuck happened to you?"

"What do you think?"

"Thought he didn't do that anymore."

"Yeah, well, so did I, sorta. Listen Rainy, you got some Vaseline or something? He would have to split my lip. How's he think I'm supposed to sing? Asshole."

"Yeah and looks like you better borrow my red lipstick too."

"Ugh."

"I know, I know, you hate red lipstick, but it honestly doesn't look bad on you and helps hide that split lip."

"I suppose."

"Gives you an excuse to wear brown or nude eye shadow to tone it down a bit, so Russo won't complain."

"Since when did he become an authority on my makeup?"

"Since he started thinking he was in charge of the band."

"He's lucky to be in the band," Mai said, rolling her eyes.

"Come on now, he's not great, but he's adequate and cheap, and he doesn't require a bigger cut for his ego," Rainy replied, laughing at her own joke.

"What's so funny?" the drummer for their jazz band, Mystical Beats, inquired as he pushed back the curtain and entered the small cubby that passed for a dressing room at the Frenchmen Street bar and bistro.

"I was just explaining how I am going to kill the first person to ask me to sing *It's a Wonderful World* tonight," said Mai.

"Just hope it's some drunk bride-to-be with a rich daddy. Weddings pay great."

"Yeah, too bad there aren't more weddings in November."

"Who wants turkey for their wedding banquet?" Rainy quipped, lifting her guitar out of its case.

"Guess I'll have to lead with Stormy Weather," Mai chuckled.

"Done. Let's get out there before the patrons get too drunk to stuff money in the tip jar on your piano and ask you to sing whatever," Russo said.

Mai took one last look in the mirror, smoothed her waist-length bleached, platinum hair and ran a finger under one green eye to erase a smear of liner and handed Rainy back her lipstick.

"Where's Armand?"

"Already on stage," Russo said.

Mai left the dressing room and headed toward the faded curtain at the end of the hall. She pushed it aside and glanced down as a tassel fell off, and stepped onto the stage, smiling in answer to Armand's nod and wink. There were already a dozen patrons, eating and drinking and ordering.

Daylight still struggled to make its way through the dirty windows that later would allow the standing room only crowds to see and hear the band from the sidewalk. Waitresses would move among them offering shots, beers and prepared hurricanes and Sazeracs in disposable plastic cups.

Once seated at the piano, she pulled the mic down and did the usual audience greeting and band intro before launching into a Billy Holiday rendition of Stormy Weather.

The bar was quickly getting crowded and louder, and the spicy scent of Creole style food made her stomach growl, reminding her that she hadn't had time to eat a proper dinner. *Everything will be closed by the time I get out of here,* she reflected. Though it wouldn't rival her Mamaw's cooking, she'd have to grab something between sets.

*****

Dozens of jazzes and bluesey songs later, Mai gave her final bow with her band members and escaped behind the heavy drapes.

"Hey, forget something?" their sax player asked, his outstretched hand holding the thick stem of the oversized snifter they used as a tip jar. It was packed tightly, and she noted with relief that there were some larger denominations among the one-and-five-dollar bills.

"Would you mind counting and divvying it up, Armand?"

"No problem, cher," he said, shrugging. His long braids swung forward, the beads clicking together. "Looks like we did okay."

"Let's hope we do even better tomorrow. Don't forget we promised to be here two hours earlier. Halloween weekend and all, it's bound to be packed all day."

"Yah, a good weekend, fer sure. Ya need me to walk you home?"

"No, I'll be fine. We're going to pick up Rainy's sister who's getting something to eat down the street."

"She still reading da tarot, ya?"

"Yeah, but they close up the street stalls at 1."

"That's right." Armand finished counting the last of the bills, grinned and handed a folded roll to Mai. "How's two c-notes sound?"

"Wow, we really did do great. Don't let Claude know or he won't want to pay us."

Armand nodded and handed rolls to Rainy and Russo.

Russo whistled and said, "Cool man, I got a date."

"At this time of night? 2:30 in the morning?" Rainy said, doing an eye roll. "Don't you mean a booty call?"

"Call it whatever you want, but I'm outta here," Russo said and headed toward the back door. Armand closed the case on his sax, grabbed it and was soon on his heels.

"You ready to blow?" Rainy asked.

Mai nodded and accompanied her down the hallway, lit with a single bare bulb dangling from the center. When she followed her through the back door, it got even darker as the only streetlight was at the far corner of the strip of businesses, mostly bars and eateries. Armand and Russo were just turning the corner from the back alley to the more brightly lit side street that ran between the last group of buildings nearest to the waterfront.

By the time the girls turned the corner the boys were long gone, but Rainy's sister Sage was headed straight for them.

"I thought I told you to wait until we got there," Rainy scolded her younger sibling.

"You just texted to tell me you were headed over," Sage retorted.

The conversation quickly turned to money, the reason the females were out here so late in the first place. Mai figured the band members were going to make 2k each this weekend, maybe more if the tips were even better tomorrow.

"My chair wasn't empty all night. Tomorrow, I plan to set up earlier and they are letting us stay open later, too," Sage said with enthusiasm. She nodded toward some inebriated tourists laughing hilariously as they stumbled down the cobblestones, drinks in hand. "Got some pretty hefty tips, too."

She went on to describe some of her more interesting clients and Mai's thoughts turned to the fact that after this weekend she would finally have enough money to make a CD of one of what they agreed was the best song she wrote with her childhood friends, Armand and Rainy. They already had their share saved up and she didn't want to let them know she had her cut ready until the money was in her hand. They'd paid for and received some great photos to use on the cover and promo stuff. They'd also bought some coordinated colored envelops in which to mail them and set them apart from other submissions.

Rainy had helped her create a database of radio hosts and managers of stations that played R & B, which was in the band's mind the best market to try to break into right now. Some of the songs Mai wrote tended to lean more toward pop or soft rock, but she loved all kinds of music and according to her band mates her two octave vocals sounded great in anything, back beats or no back beats.

She refused to feel guilty that they hadn't let Russo in on their plan. He would never have been willing to pony up his share and they all knew he had started using drugs again. Soon they'd have to replace him permanently, but for now a studio drummer would work for their initial CD. She had figured that into the cost.

They reached the coral shotgun house Rainy and Sage's Mamaw always said she bought with sweat, spit and hoodoo back in the day.

"See ya tomorrow, Mai," Sage called as she skipped onto the front stoop.

Rainy gave her a big hug and said, "You be careful."

"It's two blocks. I'll be fine," Mai assured her. She gave a final wave of her hand and headed home.

A block later, a drunk couple, who couldn't seem to decide whether to continue groping each other or swilling from the plastic cups in their hands, didn't notice her as she sidestepped into the street to avoid colliding.

Just then, a dirty black van with worn plumbing logos on the side screeched to a stop beside her. She gasped and turned to peer at the dingy windows, unable to see anything or anyone inside. She stepped back as the side doors flew open, fearing her sudden movement into oncoming traffic had startled or even angered the driver and passengers.

Mai put her hands up and said, "Sorry. I'm so sorry! I didn't mean to run into the road. I was just trying to avoid running into someone!"

The two burly men who hurtled toward her didn't seem to care about her explanation. They each grabbed an arm and began pulling her toward the van. At first, Mai was too shocked to respond, but once she realized what was happening, she flew into survival mode. She elbowed the one on her right in the gut. He grunted and released his grip, but before she could break away, he was on her again and this time his grip was tightened with rage. She wondered if Rainy could hear her from here and opened her mouth to scream. At that moment the hand of yet another assailant shoved a chemical drenched rag over her mouth.

Mai held her breath as she continued to struggle, but with three men dragging her into the van, she eventually had to breath and wasn't even aware when the van sped off down the street.

***

Her head pounded. She blinked and pushed her hair out of her face. The ceiling vaulted above her by at least twenty-five feet. It was coffered with intricate layers of dark wood and a blown glass chandelier hung from the center. She wondered where she was and then realized why she didn't know.

Bolting upright, she moaned and pressed her fingers against her temples. She swung her feet over the edge of the couch upon which she'd been dumped and tried to stand. After an initial sway and deep inhale, she managed to remain upright.

Her attention moved from the elaborate furniture to the large, expensive looking paintings on the walls, to the grand piano. She stopped when her gaze reached a plush chair to the right of the piano. The man seated in the middle of the room in what she knew was a deceptively casual manner smiled.

Mai didn't return his smile. She didn't demand to know who he was or what he wanted because she knew.

That knowledge terrified her more than the not knowing of moments before.

"Hello, Mai."

She didn't respond, but her stomach did. Her hand clamped over her mouth as she clutched her stomach.

He sprang to his feet and pointed to the double doors. "First door to the right."

Mai raced across the room, jerked the door open and burst into the bathroom down the hall. She barely made it across the room before the Po'boy she'd had for dinner landed in the toilet.

When she had nothing left in her stomach, she walked to the sink and splashed water on her face, then used her hand to cup and rinse some into her mouth. A glance in the mirror surprised her. She looked civilized, though frightened, even after the night she'd had. They must have kept their hands to themselves. Her only soreness was on her upper arms from where they manhandled her into the van. She glanced at her watch and was surprised to see it was ten. That explained why it wasn't dark outside. Had she been so heavily drugged she slept through the entire night?

She reached into her back pocket for her phone and wasn't surprised to find it gone. What did surprise her was that the two hundred was still wadded into her front pocket. A knock sounded. She wiped her face on the hand towel and taking a deep breath Mai went to open the door.

The tall, thin man she knew to be Andre Dupris held out a bottle of sparkling water, the look on his stubble-covered face almost apologetic. She wasn't the only one who'd had a long night. "They gave you too much chlorophyl. I told them to be careful, but they're obviously morons. Would you like some aspirin?"

"Yes," Mai said, but refused to say please or thank you to someone who had orchestrated her kidnapping, albeit at the behest of his boss.

She took the bottle of water and headed back to the room on her left, knowing she had no choice, at least for now.

"Ah, there you are, cher. I trust you're feeling better?"

"No thanks to you, Carlisle. I believe I have told you on numerous occasions that I am not interested."

"Please, have a seat. Your head must be throbbing. The fool who did that to you has been punished, I assure you. I would never, ever do anything to harm you, cher."

"You honestly don't think kidnapping someone would make them uninclined to believe that?"

She walked back to the couch and sat down. Carlisle spread his hands, smiling broadly. "I just want a chance to change your mind. That's all I'm asking. You want to make something of yourself, spread your beautiful voice across the country. I could make you a star practically overnight, cher. Your friends right there by your side, too."

"We never asked for your help." She knew he found it unbelievable that any female could resist his many charms. There was no denying that at six foot three the tanned Frenchman with his model-perfect cheekbones and strong jawline knew how to flash a pearly come-hither grin that melted many a young heart in New Orleans, but Mai suspected the only reason he wanted hers was that she wasn't interested. Never mind that he was arrogant and narcissistic, but he was also the head of a dangerous underground cartel, though most in New Orleans thought him just a wealthy businessman.

He didn't answer right away. Instead, he reached a slender, long-fingered hand out and grasped an elegant porcelain teacup from the small marble-topped table beside him. His amber eyes studied her over its rim as he took a deep draw. After setting it back, he said softly, "Do you think it's fair to your friends to let your stubborn pride ruin their chance for a successful music career?"

Now it was her turn to pause and consider his words. He was threatening her. It was subtle, of course. But the fact that he even knew she'd inquired about the recording studio meant he'd been checking up on her and who better to know what went on in this city? He reached across the table and picked up a large book and began flipping through the pages.

"You have to know how gorgeous you are, Mai. You're also incredibly photogenic. But then I knew you would be." He turned another page. "We must get your portrait painted."

She inhaled deeply but managed to prevent herself from gasping. He had a copy of the band's portfolio. His reach was long indeed. "We," she said with emphasis, "don't need to do anything."

"Come on now, cher, don't be difficult. I've been more than patient."

Andre chose that moment to enter with her aspirin, which she noted with amusement rested in a small paper container on a silver serving tray. She picked up the paper and tossed back the two tablets, washing them down with a swallow from the water bottle.

"Can I get you anything else?"

She shook her head, and he hurried from the room, feeling the heated gaze of his boss boring into his back. No doubt he'd gotten an earful for letting some buffoons handle her abduction.

"Are you insinuating that if I don't sleep with you, you're going to make sure my band never gets a chance to make it in the music industry? You may control New Orleans, Carlisle, but you don't control the entire country."

"I think, cher, you would be surprised how far my influence flows. However, I am not in the habit of raping women. I won't insult either one of us by pretending we don't know what my ultimate goal is, but as I said earlier, I just want a chance to convince you that I'm not as bad as you think. You just keep refusing to even give me a chance."

"And you keep refusing to realize that I mean it when I say I do not want to have a relationship with anyone right now, let alone you. I'm not in the market for a guy who will likely end up in jail for most if not all his life."

She expected him to be angry, but instead he threw back his head and laughed as though it was the funniest joke he'd ever heard.

"Oh, cher, you are the most refreshing and intriguing female I have ever met. Anyone else would be fawning over me or too terrified to respond, but you're practically spitting in my face!" And he laughed again, a deep, genuine belly laugh.

Which made Mai mad as hell. "I'm leaving," she announced and headed for the door.

"You know you won't get far. Why put yourself through the trouble and humiliation?"

She stopped and turned to face him. At least he wasn't laughing at her anymore. In fact, she looked him in the eyes and saw simmering rage there. His amusement at her defiance only went so far. He gave her a little half-grin, which lacked humor and sent fear running up her spine. He remained calm, but she'd heard from Armand, who had warned her over and over to be careful, that Carlisle was most dangerous at such times.

Mai willed herself to remain still and shoved her hands in her jean pockets so he wouldn't notice them trembling.

He stood.

She took a step back.

He took a step forward.

She locked her knees.

He moved to stand close enough for her to smell his cologne. Something expensive and woodsy with notes of oud and sandalwood. Of course he would smell good, the arrogant bastard.

But when he stuck his finger under her chin to force her to look up at him, she jerked away and before she could stop herself, she said, "Don't touch me!"

She knew it was a mistake immediately, even before he reached out to grab her around the waist and dragged her up against him. Her struggles were useless as he bent down to capture her lips with his own. Panicked and fueled with adrenaline, she managed to twist her head away and screamed, "Nooooo!"

She let it go then, the force that lived just below the surface, that dangerous part of herself that she never dared release. Fueled by the fury within her, she willed the power to wrap around his neck and she squeezed and squeezed.

Mai stumbled when he released her. He gasped and clutched his neck as if invisible hands were literally strangling him. She stared in disbelief as blood began to run out of his nostrils. His left hand clawed at his suit coat as if he couldn't breathe. His right reached up to rub his nose and then he looked at his fingers with bulging eyes. When he saw the blood, he muttered, "W-w-what d-d-did you . . ." Blood began running from his tear ducts before he collapsed at her feet.

He twitched once before she ran to the patio doors, ripped them open and ran out into the night, escaping.

***

Mai shut the cab door and ran up the steps. She dug still-shaking fingers into the dirt of the flowerpot filled with bright yellow mums and pulled out the spare key. She dropped it twice before she managed to get the door open. She locked the door behind her, slid the key onto the table beside it and hurried past the master bedroom toward the kitchen, since her bedroom was at the back of the house. She would have come in the back door if both her phone and house key hadn't been missing from her pockets.

But she'd think about that later. She had more important things to worry about right now. It wasn't her fault Carlisle apparently had a heart attack or something. It wasn't. It couldn't be.

Now she had to push the look on his face as he stared up at her, jerking at her feet...*out...of... my ...head*!

"Get it together, Mai!" She said out loud.

Rainy would be frantic since she couldn't get ahold of her. She had to hurry if she was going to shower, change, and meet Rainy at her house before they left for the bar. She had nothing in her stomach now either, so she wanted to throw together a sandwich before she left too.

In record time, she has clean, changed, sandwiched and jogging down the sidewalk as she finished the last of an apple.

Rainy and Sage met her half a block later. "Why the hell didn't you answer your phone?" Rainy demanded. "We were on our way to see if something was wrong."

"Plenty, but I'll tell you about that later," she said, with a meaningful glance at Sage.

"Oh, right, like I can't know. Must be about some man," Sage said.

"Just save your predictions for the tourists, young lady," Rainy retorted, giving Mai a *what the hell* look.

They no sooner waved goodbye to Sage and Rainy voiced her, "what the hell?"

"Carlisle."

"Him again? What now?"

"He had his goons kidnap me, chlorophyll and all last night."

Rainy stopped. She grabbed Mai's arm and said, "He didn't—"

"No, but I thought he was going to for a moment."

"So what happened? Are you okay?"

"I'm not sure. I think he might have had a heart attack or a stroke or something."

"You think?" She released her grip and added, "how did you get away?"

"As soon as he keeled over, I took off running. I climbed over the wall by standing on a garbage can and eventually saw and hailed a cab. Thankfully I still had the tip money on me. You know I never carry a purse when we have a gig."

"You don't think he'll show up tonight, do you?"

"He didn't look too good last time I saw him, so no."

"Yeah, well, I say we still have Armand walk us home. Or we call uber."

"No getting an uber at that time on this holiday weekend. I think we'll be fine."

"We'll see," Rainy said, clearly not convinced. "I'm just glad you're okay. I knew that prick was bad news."

"Yeah, I should have taken what Armand said more seriously."

From the noise level the bar was already starting to fill up when they arrived. Armand was in the dressing room, tuning his saxophone. Mai tapped Rainy on the back and when she turned to look, she shook her head. She didn't want to upset Armand until their gig was over.

She got her wish until after their first set.

Armand walked off stage and Mai followed him toward the dressing room. Russo, as usual, headed out back for a smoke, unlikely to be a cigarette. When Armand came to a stop just inside the curtain, Mai moved to go around him only to have him reach out an arm to push her back behind him.

"What's wrong?" Rainy asked, coming to a stop beside her.

She shrugged and bent to look around Armand and see what had him upset.

"Andre?" she said.

"Mai, there you are. I brought your phone and keys back to you. Could I speak to you alone for a moment?"

"No," Armand said.

"Yes," Mai said, pushing Armand aside. "Would you excuse us for a moment guys?"

"Are you sure?" Armand said, looking at her intently. "Okay, but I'll be right outside," he added, giving Andre a warning look.

What he could do about it if Andre decided to do something, Mai didn't know, but she had no intention of finding out. She waited for Armand and a gap-mouthed Rainy to move off down the hallway and walked further into the cubby. She took the phone and keys Andre held out toward her and said, "Thanks." She wasn't going to ask what he wanted. She thought it wiser to wait and see if she could expect some further trouble before stepping her foot into something.

"He's dead. I'm sure you were wondering. I don't know exactly what went on, and frankly I don't care. If it had anything to do with you, well, thanks. The autopsy report will say it was a ruptured aneurism. I'm sure you know he wasn't as well liked as he thought he was, especially by me and his, um, employees. As his what we are calling next of kin, I am his sole heir." He held out a business card. "That includes his recording studios. When you and your band go to cut your CD, tell the manager to call this number. I'm extending the courtesy discount, figuring you deserve it for all the shit Carlisle gave you. Don't look at me like that. I've got both a wife and a mistress. I'm French, but I don't need any more trouble. We're done here. For what it's worth, I wish you luck. You've got some real talent, Mai. Do N'awlin's proud."

Mai stared after Andre's retreating back. She wasn't sure what she'd expected, but not that. And what did he mean by 'if it had anything to do with her'? She hadn't done anything but wish him dead and wishes didn't kill people. They didn't. She hadn't done anything. She hadn't.

"So? What gives? Is Carlisle coming after you?" Rainy said, running into the room.

"He's still been bothering you?" Armand demanded.

"What? No. He's . . . he's dead."

"Dead?!" Rainy and Armand chorused.

"Yeah. Um, brain aneurism."

"So, what did Andre want?" Armand asked, looking between Rainy and Mai as if knowing he wasn't in this loop and not pleased about it.

"Long story short, Carlisle tried to convince me he only wanted to get to know me, but he passed out, so I took off and left my phone there and Andre returned it."

"In this case I'd say the money was in the details and I just got ripped off."

"Actually," Mai said, chuckling, "what you got is a very hefty coupon."

"Huh?" the chorus replied again.

"He took over for Carlisle and for being another person who had to put up with Carlisle's shit, he is letting us do the CD for practically cost. In case you didn't know, Carlisle owned the recording studio. So now, Andre owns it."

"No way," Rainy said. "Who would have thought having Carlisle obsessed with you would end up being a good thing."

"Ha. Ha."

"What a trip."

Russo popped his head behind the curtain and said, "You guys coming or what?"

"Yup, be right there," Mai said.

***

Mai's bedroom was at the back of the colorful shotgun house, just behind the kitchen. Thankful for having her key back so she wouldn't have to creep past Mamaw's room, she tossed it onto her dresser and opened the little top drawer to stuff the three hundred in tips she got tonight.

She walked through to the kitchen to get a snack and noticed that the little light over the sink wasn't on. It was unlike Mamaw not to leave a light on for her when she worked late.

Just then she heard the front doorknob rattle. She grabbed a knife from the magnetic strip and hurried past the table to duck down into the shadows, laser-focused on the front door. The porch light was on, and she stood and relaxed once she realized who was there, if not why.

"Where were you at this time of night, Mamaw?" she asked, setting the knife down.

"Oh, you startled me, Mai." She put her purse and keys on the table beside the door and locked the door behind her. "I'm glad you're here. We need to talk, sha."

"Is something wrong?"

Mamaw walked over to her and turned on the light above the table. "Have a seat, Mai."

Mai sat down and waited patiently. Something was terribly wrong. She clutched her hands together in her lap.

"I just came from the hospital. It's Renard. He's dead. He had a stroke at work today, and he didn't make it."

"What?" Mai stood up and stepped over to her Mamaw's chair and quickly stooped down to wrap her arms around her. "Are you okay?"

"I'm fine." She seemed distracted, as if she had a bigger problem than that her husband just died. Then, looking at Mai, she said, "Oh, about Renard. Yes, fine, fine. I knew it was going to happen, just not quite so soon. But he brought it on himself."

"How? What are you talking about? You knew he was going to die? You mean the way you knew when--"

They both turned to look at the front door.

"Who could that be?" Mai asked.

Mamaw didn't respond, but instead hurried to the front door. Mai realized she had expected the knock as she didn't even look through the peep hole before opening the door.

Whoever it was murmured something Mai didn't hear before her Mamaw shook her head and said, "Not yet. I was just about to."

She stepped back and the mysterious visitor moved inside.

"Marraine?" Mai said, surprised. She walked over to give her godmother a hug. She hadn't seen her since her coming-of-age celebration.

"Come, sha, yer Mamaw say she 'bout to tell ya something 'portant. We go sit. The old woman didn't wait for a response but moved to enthrone herself in an overstuffed armchair.

Mai looked at her Mamaw in confusion but obeyed the silent command to sit on the couch next to her. She knew better than to question her mother in front of her clan's Marraine. She worried her bottom lip, realized it when she disturbed the mostly healed split, and stopped.

"Mai. I know what Renard did to you."

"What he did?"

"I know he hit you when I was at work. He told me about it. I think he assumed you would have told me. He said he was sorry and that he had apologized and that it would never happen again."

"Yes, yes he did apologize." *Is this what is so important?* Mai thought.

"Mai, I want you to consider carefully about your reaction to that. Even if you didn't backtalk him, and I'm sure you didn't. What were you thinking?"

"I-I was angry."

"Yes, of course you were. But what exactly did you think? You might not have meant it, but did you wish him harm in any way?"

Mai fisted her hand and pressed it against her chest. She shook her head and closed her eyes, remembering. It couldn't have been her. It couldn't. That was crazy. Was Mamaw suggesting that she harmed Renard? Did she hurt Carlisle too? That wasn't possible. Wishing didn't make things happen. It just didn't. Or did it? Did it?

She opened her eyes and gazed intently at her Mamaw. "Are you suggesting that my angry thoughts brought harm to Renard? To Carlisle?"

"Carlisle? Explain. What happened, Mai? Tell me exactly what happened with Carlisle. Are you talking about Carlisle Boissau?" She exchanged a look with the Marraine.

"He died," she said softly. "I wished he didn't even exist, that he would get out of my life and leave me alone. I imagined how great it would be to just choke the life out of him. But I never touched him. I swear. But then, blood started to come out of his mouth and then his eyes and then he fell to the floor. And, and I ran away so I don't know what all happened, but I was told he died."

"Ah. You knew, didn't you? You felt it. You knew."

Tears welled in Mai's eyes. Mamaw was right. Somehow, she did know that she hurt Carlisle. She denied it at the time, refusing to even think about it. But now she recalled the complete frustration and rage he ignited in her and how at the very moment she wished he would drop dead, blood began flowing from his nostrils, and then his eyes. His eyes. Seeing blood running from his eyes looked like something from a horror movie. She ran but not just because she wanted to escape. She ran because she knew. She knew what she had done. Andre knew too. And Mamaw. And the Marraine? Is that why she was here at 4 am while it was not yet light?

"But nothing happened with Renard. You were here. And he went to work the next day, so it wasn't anything I did."

"Spec ya weren't so mad at dat Renard." She turned to Mamaw and said, "Tol ya da man be a bastard."

Looking back at Mai, she said, "It were a slow push what simmered and growed in em an took time ta work."

"A push? But I never pushed him."

"You pushed your intention on him, your anger, Mai," Mamaw said softly. She reached out and took Mai's hand. "I should have prepared you for this. The Marraine wanted me to, but I foolishly wanted you to enjoy your life, to be more carefree than I was allowed to be. At least for a while longer I wanted you to think you were, well, like your friends."

"So, what am I then? Am I like you? You have the sight. I heard Marraine say it once. And you know things, like before they happen."

"I kept you from developing those abilities. I guess now I shouldn't have kept any of it from you."

Mai thought back to the little voodoo shop Marraine owned over on what she still called Lavee Street even though Rue de la levee had been called Decatur since 1870. But the old folks had been calling it levee for generations. The stuff up front, most of that junk was for tourists. Folks knew the tarot card and tea leaf readers over there weren't just for tourists though.

Her Mamaw worked there when she was Mai's age. When Mai was little, it used to fascinate her. But in the back, in the area only a select few and other clan members were allowed, there were things in there that scared her. She could sense something, some mysterious power that emanated from that area. Marraine emanated power too.

She felt a jolt, like an electric shock passed from her Mamaw's hand to her own. Looking up into her eyes, a paler shade of green than her own emerald ones, they held a sheen, almost a glow, as if lit from within.

Marraine stood and walked over to stand before them. "Gimme ya hand, sha."

Mamaw released it immediately, and Mai obediently placed her hand within Marraine's. Again, the static zap passed through her hand. It wasn't painful, just surprising. Centuries of a culture that respected their elders, and their ancestors, and their clan leaders kept her hand where it had been ordered to be.

"She be da one. Tol' ya." She shook her head. "Tol' ya, Louisa Mai. Time be wasted. So much wasted. Da ritual tomarra," Marraine said.

Mai glanced at her Mamaw who nodded in agreement. *The one what?* she wondered, but didn't dare ask. *And what friggin' ritual?*

"Bring 'er tomarra." Without another word, Marraine headed toward the exit. Mamaw scrambled to get ahead of her and open the door.

"Thanks for coming, Marraine. Sorry for the trouble," Mamaw said, bobbing her head respectfully.

The moment the door shut, Mai said, "Mamaw, what the hell is going on? Am I in trouble? Did I really kill someone? I didn't mean to, I swear."

"Hush, child. You're not in trouble. It's my fault, not yours. I should have trained you."

"Trained me in what?" Although she'd asked, Mai wasn't sure she wanted to know. Worse yet, she suspected that she already knew. She'd heard whispers. Cousins and other clan children had told her stories over the years. She was born and raised in Nola. She knew a thing or two about magic and . . . other things.

"Sit down. Marraine is mad at me, not you," she assured her. She patted the couch next to her and Mai sat down.

She felt tired of a sudden, bone weary.

"What does she mean when she says I'm the one?"

"In the future, the near future, your star will rise, Mai. You will be uniquely positioned to help our people and protect our culture. The world is changing. The Marraine and I know it. We've become fossils."

"Mamaw, you're 45 years old. Hardly a fossil. And what do you mean about my star rising?" She couldn't disguise her sudden excitement. "Do we make it? Does my band make it big?"

"That's what draws your attention from all that's going on?"

She was right. Mai knew it. The point being made was about responsibility for her family, her people, not personal success. It was about taking responsibility for what she had done to two grown men folk, whether she meant to or not.

Selfishness wasn't how she had been raised. She hung her head, knowing she had been given incredible personal freedom to make her own choices, even though her Mamaw frequently reminded her that once she was grown there would be a lot of people who depended on her. Whenever she asked what Mamaw meant, she had been told to never mind, you'll know when the time is right.

That time was now.

Whether she was ready or not.

***

Mai pulled the collar of her jacket up. She wasn't ready to completely forgive Rainy and Armand. Not yet. She understood why they never told her. She did. But she wasn't ready to forget them yet.

Rainy wrapped her arm around Mai's waist. "I really am sorry, Mai. You know I love you, right?" she whispered.

Mai knew Mamaw, seated ahead of them in the small boat, could hear and only pretended not to.

"I know. And I will forgive you, but I'm still feeling a little betrayed. You guys are my besties. I trusted you."

"You still can. I swear. Your Mamaw wanted you to have some fun, to not have to worry about it yet, and so my Mamaw forbade me to tell you. The grown folks talked it through and decided. Weren't none of our doing."

Armand had said much the same thing. Armand and Rainy weren't blood kin. But they had been closer than that to Mai. To her they were heart kin, as well as her clan.

Clan kinship had a hierarchy, like a family, and they all had to obey the Marraine, since the Parrain passed. If she said Mamaw could keep the truth from Mai until the vision she'd seen came to pass, then so be it.

The fact that Renard's passing was that vision disturbed Mai as much as anything else. How could Mamaw keep that from her? She claimed nothing she said or did would have prevented it, because her visions always came true no matter what. Unfortunately, Mai knew that was true and had been true all her life.

She had to do as Mamaw said or would surely regret it, which is why she sat in this flat-bottomed boat deep in the Louisiana bayou on her way to a ritual in which she would be the guest of honor.

Tonight she would be indoctrinated as her clan's future Marraine, and in order to do that, she must attend this ritual. She had no choice, because she was going to fulfill a prophecy I which she would become the most powerful Marraine who had ever yet been born.

Mamaw said it would happen, so it would. She also claimed Mai was going to be a huge music star and make millions of dollars that would help their people survive some horrible future catastrophe.

The clan never was as strong after Katrina. Mamaw saw it coming and everyone was warned, so none died. But some lost their homes. If she'd been blessed with a beautiful voice and other mystical gifts to help her kinfolk and her clan folk, she would do her best to prove worthy—no matter how terrified she felt. From childhood they were taught to take pride in their heritage. To do otherwise was unthinkable.

"Mamaw said you'll feel more confident and know a lot of stuff, magic stuff, after the ritual," Rainy said.

"That's true," Armand said softly, from the back of the boat where he operated the softly humming small trolling motor.

Mai remained silent. The swamp was beautiful at night. The moon was a mere sliver tonight, but the lanterns on the boat gleamed off the water and the occasional creatures they encountered. The gators eyed them with suspicion, but the bullfrogs serenaded them. Any other time, Armand would be itching to snatch them up for some tasty legs.

The lantern hanging from a post in front of the boat and another on a swivel lever on the rear provided Armand as much light as he needed to navigate. He'd been here countless times, both day and night. They were headed toward the ancestral cemetery. It was a familiar place to them all.

Mai watched low-hanging moss sway in the evening breeze. She usually found it romantic, but tonight it appeared almost sinister. She started when a large owl flapped into the air to pursue his dinner.

To distract her, Mamaw pointed to the right, up ahead. "Look there, do you think it a restless spirit or the location of treasure?"

"Swamp gas, most like," Mai said. "Look further over. A lot of it here. Unless there's a sunk Spanish galleon way out here in the bayou, I'd say swamp gas. Any spirits will be awaiting me ahead."

Rainy laid her head on Mai's shoulder.

"It's okay, Rainy. I need to get control of this thing. This-this power. I can't chance hurting anyone." *Anyone else*, she thought to herself.

***

Mai laid the basket of mangoes before Parrain's monument, keeping one back. Then she handed Mamaw the spiced rum. She walked over to the small marker on her papere's grave and laid the single mango. Papere liked apples better and she reached into her pocket and produced a big red one. "Chosen special just for you, Papere," she said softy. "Watch out for me tonight." She made a quick stop to visit Mawmaw and Pawpaw, side by side as they so often were in life. She barely remembered her kin, having all passed when she was very young.

"Come, sha," Marraine called.

She looked over to see her Mamaw already standing beside her, along with their kin and clan folk, forming a rather large outer circle and a smaller circle within, made up of immediate family and her heart's kin, Rainy and Armand. A rather large bonfire warmed them and lit their faces, casting their features in misshapen shadows and flickering burnt orange highlights.

Walking up, she took the cup Mamaw handed to her. "Drink it all quickly, sha."

With all eyes on her, she downed the amber liquid, swallowing the vile, burning concoction and promptly coughed over and over. Mamaw patted her on the back.

The rum, spice and herbs she knew would help send her into a trance-like state. It would help her more easily receive the gifts, mystical powers her ancestors were safeguarding for her, having anxiously waited for this very moment, some for centuries.

Mamaw explained as best she could what she should expect, but Mamaw had never been given full power. She hadn't been chosen by the ancestors. For some reason, Mai was the chosen one. Nothing could have prepared her. She didn't even know how to describe what she felt almost at once—what she heard and smelled.

Her head felt heavy and fell forward. Her lids felt heavy, and her eyes closed. She smelled Papere's pipe. She didn't know how she realized or even remembered that sweet aroma of cherry and vanilla. But then she smelled Lily of the Valley, her Mawmaw's favorite scent. The smells and impressions came so fast after that she didn't always understand who or what they represented. She heard voices, so many voices, all giving her information that she somehow understood and remembered. Spells. Curses. Alchemy. Rituals. Centuries of hoodoo and voodoo and even ancient knowledge she doubted the current Marraine knew.

Then her body went stiff as if she were a conduit and lightning coursed through her body. Her head fell back. Her eyes flew open and then she could no longer see the physical world around her because her eyes rolled back in her head.

She heard her Mamaw cry out her name, but she seemed to get further and further away. The ground no longer felt solid under her feet and some portion of her mind realized she was levitated above her family and clan members.

Her entire body tingled and what she saw was another time and another place. Large stones surrounded her, and they were no longer a grouping of graves but a circle of large, arranged boulders that encircled a single grave, the grave of a king or ruler of some kind. Robed men carrying torches chanted within what she knew to be a sacred place.

Information continued to flood her mind with the memories and knowledge of hundreds of ancestors. She zapped from one sacred ceremony to another and another until finally the visions slowed.

Then stopped.

Slow but steady her body drifted back down to earth, but her thoughts still overwhelmed her. She stumbled back from the fire, wiping at sweat now beading on her brow. Taking the bottle of water Mamaw thrust into her hand, she guzzled half of it. Then, sucking in gulps of air, she said, "No way was I ready for that, Mamaw."

"Are you okay? Are you hurt anywhere? Does your head hurt?"

"Give da child a few to gather dem thoughts. Her brain be plum full," cautioned the Marraine.

"I'm-I'm exhausted," Mai said. "I'd like to go home and get some rest."

"Sure, sha. Visit me da shop when ya feel ready."

Her kin gathered around her then, each of them giving her a hug or patting her back, but she realized they thought they were getting luck as if she were a living gris-gris rather than offering comfort.

She supposed they were right.

Tired as she was, she murmured a blessing, given to all those present, a spell gifted to her by a young woman who lived three centuries ago, a young woman who was burned at the stake.

She died in agony, but gave this gift to her descendent, Mai, with a smile, because she too was a witch.

UNHOLIER THAN THOU

Darren Simon

Mary returned home from church, her heart racing faster and faster. She pulled her SUV into the driveway, her stomach rock hard, her lungs tight. She could barely manage a shallow breath. Bringing her vehicle to a stop, she peered through the windshield at her son's upstairs window. An icy chill spread through her body. She blinked back tears.

"God, give me strength." She closed her eyes and forced a deep breath. "Please, Lord, help me to save him."

From the passenger seat, she lifted a plastic bag. Inside were a Bible, a bronze crucifix and a small flask filled with holy water she'd snuck from the church. She lifted the Bible from the bag and studied the worn, slightly bent cover. It was black with gold lettering that read, *The King James Bible.* She clutched it to her chest, then kissed the cover. *This must work. It just must.* She again kissed the Bible and then exited the vehicle.

A raspy, icy voice echoed in her head. *"It won't work, Mommy. I belong to him, now."*

"No." She held a fist toward the air. Her body trembled despite her thick beige overcoat, but not because of the gray, cold afternoon. "You can't take him." With her free hand, she reached into her coat pocket. Her fingers wrapped around the handle of a dagger she'd just purchased at Ray's Hunting Supplies.

Taking one more painful deep breath, she crossed from the driveway along the paved red brick walkway lined with flowers and covered with large orange leaves, making her way to the front door.

She stopped at the steps leading up the porch. A gasp escaped her lips.

Blood seeped through the bottom of the door, pooling onto the porch, covering her son's handprint from when he was a baby. They had just poured the concrete then for the doorway of their new house on Eugene Street in the quiet Upstate New York neighborhood they'd chosen as their home.

Mary screamed in silence. She ran up the steps and tried to open the door. It wouldn't budge. Her mind raced. She hadn't locked it when she kissed her husband goodbye and urged him to watch over Nicholas. She fumbled through her purse for her keys. Gripping the keychain, she yanked it free only to drop the keys into the blood.

"David," she called to her husband. She pounded one fist against the door, but no one responded. Bending down, she scooped up the keys. Blood coated her fingers, but she still managed to insert the key into the lock. One hand pushing on the door, she tried to turn the key, but it wouldn't move. "David, let me in. Please, for the love of God." She twisted the knob over and over, but the door was jammed. "David... Dav—"

The lock finally clicked. The door gave way. Mary pushed through only to trip over something, her hands and knees landing on gray tile soaked in blood. The plastic bag she carried flew out of her hand. She craned her neck to see the source—and covered her mouth. Jasper, their son's golden retriever, lay like a bag of trash near the door, his head twisted unnaturally, blood seeping from his neck and torso.

Flies swarmed the dog. Where the hell had the flies come from? Already, the stench of rotting flesh rose from Jasper's broken body. Mary's insides convulsed. Spew climbed her throat. She couldn't hold it back. Her chest heaved, and the vomit came.

When it was over, she sucked in air and peered up at the front door. Jagged lines of blood slid down the wall just above the entryway and dripped onto the door. Mary followed them with her eyes, violently shaking her head and tugging her hair. Someone had scratched the words "Doggy Dead" in a splattering of blood on the wall high above the door.

"David, where are you?" Panting, Mary picked herself up, wiping her blood-stained hands on her coat. She swung around, searching for the plastic bag, then spotted it by the coffee table. Grabbing it, making sure the Bible, crucifix and holy water were still inside, she started up the stairs. "David, answer me."

The last item she checked for was the dagger inside her coat. She sighed. It was still there.

The deep, raspy voice, with just a hint of her son's gentleness, again echoed in her head. *"Hurry, Mommy, come and see."*

"Nicholas, I'm coming." She climbed the last stair and reached her son's room. "Everything will be all right. David, are you in there?"

"We're waiting, Mommy." The voice on the other side was fully her son's now but from when he was four or five years old, and he was nine now. He hadn't called her mommy for years. *"Come and see what we've done to Daddy."*

Mary's body trembled. Her insides froze. She softly placed the palms of her hands against her son's door. "Why is this happening?" Her hands slid down the door until they reached the doorknob. The metal was so frigid it burned her skin, but she didn't let go. She closed her eyes and began to utter a prayer she learned as a child. "Though I walk through the valley of the shadow of death, I will fear no evil..."

She opened the door. Her eyes bulged. Her heart slammed against her chest. Terror stole her ability to scream. *No, David,* she mouthed.

Her husband hovered above Nicholas' bed, his arms held aloft as if he'd been crucified. Blood seeped from his palms. His legs were bent and twisted around each other, like a raggedy doll. His head hung loosely against his chest, nothing but the whites of his eyes visible. An eerie smile parted his lips.

"Do you like what we've done, Mommy?" The voice came from beside her.

Mary's stare slowly shifted to her side. This time she unleashed a shriek. Nicholas stood next to her, head craned back almost to the point of snapping off his neck. He glared at her upside down. His thick, wavy blond hair had nearly fallen out, leaving nothing but a few strands against his balding, puss-covered head.

He stood shirtless with only pajama pants, soiled and barely clinging to his thin frame. Mary's mouth opened wide. Her legs nearly crumbled. The words *He's Mine Now* were carved into his stomach.

Mary reached for him but recoiled.

She was losing her sweet boy.

"Mommy, what's the matter? Does our artwork not please you?" Nicholas sneered at her with raven black eyes surrounded by a sea of red. Bloody tears slid down bone-thin cheeks, his skin torn and hanging from the sides of his face. He smiled wide, revealing yellow jagged teeth. Mary shook her head. *Oh, God, where's my son? Nicholas, come back to me.*

Nicholas grabbed her hand, wrapping bony fingers around hers. He squeezed until it hurt. She cringed but didn't try to break his grip.

"Mommy, why don't you answer us?" His eyes widened; his twisted smile nearly split his face in half.

Mary couldn't hold back her hot tears. "Nicholas, please release your father."

"Nicholas is gone, Mommy. We are what remains." The voice that spoke was deep and phlegmy. Green ooze dripped from the sides of her son's mouth. His head twisted upright, but his black eyes remained locked on her, even as he crossed to his bed and slid underneath the covers.

"Nicholas, ple—"

"As you wish, Mommy." Nicholas pointed a finger at his father. David's arms dropped to his side, and then his entire body collapsed to the floor. He didn't move. He just lay there, his body bent and twisted, eyes still rolled up into his head.

Crusty breaths limped out of his throat. Mary cradled his mangled body in her lap and held his head to her chest. "David, no, don't leave me." He hissed out one final breath and then was silent.

"David," Mary cried. "David."

She rocked him in her shaking arms. Crazed laugher, like a chicken squawking, came from her son.

"Shut up, you bastard." Mary's gaze shot from the plastic bag she'd dropped on the floor with the Bible, crucifix and holy water, to her pant pocket. In a heartbeat, she made her choice. She ripped the dagger from her pocket. "Damn you."

She lunged at her son the dagger raised over her head. Landing on top of him, she grabbed his neck with her free hand and aimed the dagger at his heart. "I'll rip you out of my son, you son of a bitch."

"Mom, no." Her son uttered the words in his actual voice. His eyes shifted from coal black to light blue, his natural color. *"Mom, it's me. Help me, please. Don't kill me."* In that instant, the beast inside vanished. His

blond hair returned, and his skin healed. *"Mom, please."* He reached up to her with shaky arms.

Mary gazed at her son. Her heart softened. She released her grip on his neck. Her hand holding the dagger dropped to her side; the blade slid from her fingers and dropped to the floor. "Oh, my Nicholas."

She scooped him into her arms, his head resting on her shoulder. "Nicholas, I love you. I would never—"

The crazed laugher returned.

Mary grabbed his shoulders and shoved him an arm's distance away. The beast inside had returned. Black eyes glared at her. Green, foamy puss slid from open wounds in his cheeks. A twisted smile crossed his face.

She shook her head and mouthed the word, "no," over and over. Any flame of hope inside extinguished, replaced by an emptiness that made it hard to breathe. "Nicholas, fight this."

"Nicholas is mine now, Mommy." The beast's voice returned. *"He asked for this, but you can still be our mommy."*

Mary backed away, her eyes searching for the dagger. "No, never."

"Then get out and leave us be." Her son thrust his arms at her, palms up.

An invisible sledgehammer smashed into her. She flew backward, her arms and legs flailing uselessly. With a thwack, she collided with the bedroom door, jolting her head forward, then back. White hot pain flashed before her eyes, blinding her. The door gave way, flinging her into the hallway. Gasping for a breath, she tumbled down the stairs, her body rolling over and over until she no longer felt anything—until darkness overtook her.

***

In the distance came the rumble of thunder. A burst of light squeezed through her closed eyelids, then came the crack of more thunder, this time so loud it shook the house. Mary's eyes fluttered open. Consciousness returned. Her head pounded in rhythm with the beat of her heart. Dizziness made her stomach churn. Though they felt heavy, her eyes fully opened. More thunder rattled the house. She flinched.

She lay on her back at the base of the stairs but how long? It had to be hours. Night had fallen. The house was cloaked in darkness, save for one flickering light in the upstairs hallway that sent shadows dancing along the staircase. The house stunk, like trash left out in the heat. She peered toward the door. Jasper's rotting body lay there, a meal for the flies buzzing throughout the living room.

Shivering, each breath forming a mist that slid from her mouth, Mary rubbed her arms to generate warmth.

She slowly turned herself onto her side. She could barely pull herself up. Every muscle screamed in protest. Pain radiated from the back of her skull, and when she ran her fingers through her hair front to back, her fingertips found a gash. Yelping, she moved her hand in front of her face. Blood dripped from her fingertips.

Blinking rapidly, sucking in the chilled air, she forced away the last bits of haziness and ignored the pain. She had to kill the beast; she had to save her son.

She lifted herself onto her knees.

"Mary, why did you let this happen?" The voice was David's, but he was…

She let that thought trail off. Her gaze climbed the stairs one step at a time. Her breath lodged in her throat. Her pulse quickened.

"Mary, why?"

"David," she wailed. Her husband hovered at the top of the stairs, his feet dangling just above the floor. Under the dim flickering light, he seemed more shadow than flesh. His arms hung uselessly at his side. Mary held a hand to her racing heart. She stood on shaky legs, eyes locked on her husband. David's head tilted to one side. Black goo slid from between his lips, which parted in an eerie smile. *David, no.* His eyes had been ripped from his face.

"David, I'm sorry." Mary shielded her eyes and backed away with jerky steps.

"You let this happen. You didn't keep our son safe. You let this happen to me. Look at me, Mary. Look at what you've done." Mary peered at him through her fingers. Her husband's body started down the stairs.

"No, David." Mary turned away, scrambling through the living room, tripping over the coffee table and nearly falling to the floor. Managing to stay on her feet, she stumbled to the front door.

Raspy laughter echoed through the house. The walls shook. Cabinet doors flew open. A glass chandelier fell from the ceiling shattering across the floor.

"Stop it." She grabbed the doorknob and twisted it over and over, her arms straining to force it open. She wheezed out shallow breaths until her lungs burned. Sweat covered her palms, making it impossible to grip the doorknob.

She sobbed wildly. "David, I'm sorry. I'm so sorry."

With one final push, she thrust the door open… and crumbled outside into the arms of a shadowy figure standing just outside her door.

She unleashed a primal scream and thrashed her arms. A flash of lightning allowed her a glimpse of the stranger's face. He was tall with narrow cheeks and a thin layer of gray hair. The lightning revealed one more detail—the white priestly collar around his neck.

Lightning gave way to thunder. The stranger didn't react. He held her gently until she was steady. He then bowed to her. "Bonjour, my good lady. I'm sorry for this intrusion, but I believe you are in need of assistance. I am Father Luca Prieto, an emissary of the Pope, and I've been sent on behalf of the Church. Word has reached the Holy Father that you have a child in the throes of a possession."

Mary stepped back until she struck the doorframe. Her mind spun wildly. She hunched over, struggling to breathe. What had this stranger just said? All she could really hear was the loud pounding of her heart.

She tried to speak but couldn't utter a word. "Wh… wh… who—"

"Madame, I have been sent to help." He took a step closer to the door. Another spark of lightning revealed his gray eyes and thick white eyebrows that nearly touched. "Might I pardon you to invite me in, so that we might begin."

Mary peered back through the door. There was no sign of her dead husband. She trembled anyway. Had she imagined it? Maybe all of this was just a nightmare, and she'd wake up soon to make her husband and sweet son breakfast. No, this was more than just a nightmare. She'd lost everything.

She turned back to the stranger and found some words. "Father, help my son."

"I will try." He spoke kindly with a deep voice, offering a slight smile and extending a hand with long, thin fingers. Mary studied his hand. An image of a cross was tattooed into his palm. She cautiously grasped his hand. It was rough and icy.

One thought raced through her mind. How was it possible the Church knew of her son? She told no one, just like her husband had demanded.

She let go of his hand. How could she trust this stranger? Then again, what choice did she have?

"Madame, I implore you, the storm is getting worse in these early morning hours, and these old bones would very much appreciate the chance to come in where it's warm. Perhaps I might even do some good."

Lightning streaked across the sky. "Will you please invite this old servant of the Lord into your home?"

Mary relented. She'd begged God for help, and maybe this old priest was the answer to her prayers. "Yes, Father, please come inside, but you'll find no warmth here."

***

Farther Prieto again bowed and stepped across the threshold, beyond the door and into the living room. Mary watched his every move. He walked gracefully with a black cane topped by a golden handle in the shape of a…. Mary shivered and wrapped her arms around her body. Were her eyes deceiving her? His cane was topped by a golden carving of a wolf's head. In his other hand, he carried a plain brown satchel with scratch marks on both sides. *Is this really a priest*? A long black trench coat covered what seemed to be a very thin frame judging by a face where his pale skin clung tightly to his bones.

His gaze focused on the dead dog, and he shook his head. "They always kill the dog. I see no point in it."

"Excuse me?" Mary kept her distance. Why in the hell was he commenting on Jasper? Her husband was dead. Her little boy had become a beast.

Father Prieto waved his cane at the flies circling around them. His face turned grim. Lines spread across his forehead. "These damned demons. They always seem to kill the family dog first. It's a pity."

Mary's hands balled into fists. "Father, my husband is dead. My son, who's possessed by God knows what, killed him."

"My lady, God does know what has befallen your family, as do I." Father Prieto slowly lowered into a rocking chair, then put down his cane and satchel beside the chair. He rubbed his hands together, blew on them and started to slowly rock back and forth, the chair squeaking with each movement.

"Father, please." Mary stood over him, clasping her fingers under her chin.

He nodded. "I am very sorry for your loss, but you must not think your son is to blame. It is the beast inside."

Mary peered up the stairs through the flickering light. "You mean, Satan?"

Father Prieto chuckled. "Heavens no. The father of hell has no reason to possess a human. No, your son, I believe, is possessed by a demon, unless he's just gone mad and in doing so has gained supernatural abilities. I've seen that before, but I don't believe this is the case."

Mary grasped her head with both hands. Nothing made sense anymore. "How do you know any of this? How does the Church know about my son? Explain that. We never reached out for help. My husband didn't believe our son was possessed. He just thought—"

Father Prieto motioned for her to sit on the nearby couch. The flies still buzzed him, but he ignored them. "You should have sought help, my lady. Perhaps I could have responded sooner, but I flew in soon as I could, as soon as I sensed—"

"I don't understand." Mary lowered to her knees and grasped Father Prieto's hands.

He gently held hers, patting the top of her hand like a consoling parent. Mary took note that both of his palms had the marking of the cross. "Madame, the Holy Father sent me to help in hope that I might make a difference in your son's case, if we are not too late. You see, I'm the lead exorcist for the Roman diocese and advisor to the Holy Father himself on demonology."

She sunk into the couch across from him and buried her head in her hands. She started to sob again. "How is any of this possible? This isn't supposed to be real."

Father Prieto leaned forward. "My lady, it is all real. The things that go bump in the night. The sensation of fear you get when you feel someone is watching you. It's all real. Something evil is always close at hand. Satan, demons, monsters… they are all real. Our best defense is our faith in God. It's really all we have."

Mary gazed up with reddened eyes. "Can you save my son?"

Father Prieto slowly stood. His knees cracked and shook with the effort. He then reached for his cane and satchel. "That's what I am here to try to do, but I can make no promises. Now, show me to your son's room."

"This way." Mary tried to lift herself from the couch, but her body protested. Her head ached from the fall. Pain snaked up her back, wrapping around her shoulders and her neck, like invisible tentacles squeezing her body. Bile rose up her throat, but she forced it down. Now was not the time to be sick.

One more time, she forced her body to rise. This time, her limbs listened. Grasping onto the banister with both hands, she trudged up the stairs on burning legs. She stopped when lightning flashed outside followed by the rumble of thunder. The chill around her worsened with each step. It hurt to breathe. The white mist pouring from her nose and mouth with each labored breath thickened, but she didn't stop. "I'm bringing help, Nicholas."

Crazed laughter echoed from her son's room, rattling the house. The stairs shook violently. Mary almost lost her balance but Father Prieto, right behind her, placed a hand on her shoulder.

The beast's raspy voice echoed around her. *"Mommy, the boy is mine now. It's what he wanted. It's what he asked for. No priest can separate us. We love you, Mommy. Come take care of us. Don't let the bad priest hurt us."*

Mary bit her lower lip until she tasted the saltiness of her own blood. She dropped to one knee. "No, Nicholas is my son. You can't have him."

Father Prieto stood over her. "Steady, my lady, the demon knows how to weaken you. Harden your heart to his words."

Picking herself up, Mary continued to climb, but with each step her legs felt heavier, like her feet were sinking into mud. Near the top of the staircase, the lights stopped flickering. Darkness surrounded her. She paused for just a heartbeat, then took the next step and the next, but the second floor seemed to be getting farther away. Her vision tunneled. The staircase spiraled. A cold sweat spread across her brow.

The only sound was a quiet chant from Father Prieto, who walked right behind her. She recognized the song from her childhood. *"Jesus loves me—this I know, For the Bible tells me so."* She remembered how the song would bring her comfort when she was a little girl. Somehow, hearing Father Prieto chant it made the little hairs on her arm stand.

"Madame, can you continue?" Father Prieto asked.

She shook her head. "Yes, Father."

He leaned in closer to her until his lips were not far from her ear and whispered. "Do not fear the dark. It is not the enemy of light. Our God is just as powerful in the darkness as He is in the light. Remember that."

Mary didn't look back at Father Prieto. She shuddered. She'd never heard those words before.

Finally, they reached the top of the stairs and crossed to Nicholas' room. She placed her ear to his door, but only silence greeted her. Where was the maniacal laughter? Why had the beast stopped talking to her? She turned toward Father Prieto. "I don't hear him anymore. My God, are we too late?"

Father Prieto frowned. "No madame, I can sense both your son and the beast on the other side of this door." He tapped her shoulder with his cane. "What is about to happen is a fight for your son's life. You must be strong because I believe it is important for you to be in there with me. Are you ready for what we're about to face?"

Mary sighed. Her insides were hollow. She had almost no strength left. Her legs could barely support her. "I'll do what I have to for my son."

Father Prieto smiled slightly. "I know you will. Now let's begin."

***

Father Prieto was the first to step into Nicholas' room. Mary took a deep breath and followed. The room, like the rest of the house, was shrouded in darkness. Black muck was splattered across the walls. The stench of foul-smelling vomit, like filth left to simmer in a toilet, made her gag. She covered her mouth and held her stomach.

Her eyes immediately found her husband's twisted body in the corner. He lay there, like a boneless pile of skin. She shook her head. Her mind twisted in every direction. *See*, she told herself. It had been her imagination. He hadn't attacked her from the stairs. David would never do that. *He loved—*

Her husband's head twisted toward her. He smiled wide at her with vacant eye sockets. *"Mary, you allowed this."*

She screamed.

Father Prieto turned toward her. "Madame, what is it?"

She pointed toward her dead husband, but he no longer smiled at her. His head faced the wall.

Father Prieto raised a grey eyebrow. "We must keep our wits about us if we are to save your son."

He swung back toward Nicholas' bed, which was empty, save for sheets torn to shreds and covered in black ooze. "I do not see your—"

"Here I am priest." The raspy, phlegmy words came from behind them.

Mary peered over her shoulder and gasped. "Nicholas."

Her son, naked, his skin green and torn, pieces hanging from his chest and stomach, crawled along the ceiling. His head was unnaturally twisted as if no longer attached to his neck.

Mary grabbed on to Father Prieto's shoulder. "Please help him."

"Yes priest, save us." Nicolas opened his mouth wide. Spew flew from between his lips, splashing across Father Prieto's face. Mary turned her head away and when she looked back, Father Prieto removed a handkerchief from his coat pocket and calmly wiped away the vomit.

The beast laughed and crawled from the ceiling to the wall, then leaped to the floor in front of the Father. Nicholas' black eyes never blinked. More spew dribbled from his lips. He tore out a few strands of what hair remained atop the boy's head. *"You cannot save us, can you? You know the boy and I are one now."*

Father Prieto crossed to a nightstand. He placed his satchel on top of it and then turned back to the demon, both hands atop the wolf-head shaped handle of his cane. "Demon, I've battled many of your kind before. This fight has only just begun. Before this night is over, the boy and this world will be rid of you one way or another."

Mary glanced at him. Her body trembled. Mist rose with each breath. What did he mean, *one way or the other?*

Father Prieto turned from the beast, reached into his satchel and removed two black gloves, which he carefully slid over each hand.

"Priest, what game shall we play tonight?" Nicholas, crawling on all fours, inched closer to him. "I so enjoy warping the weak minds of servants like yourself, and then granting you a merciful death when you beg me for it."

Father Prieto didn't respond. His hands covered by gloves, he reached back into his satchel and lifted out a wooden crucifix and a glass container filled with liquid. Mary presumed it to be holy water, just like she had taken from her church. She lowered her head. In a moment of rage earlier, she'd chosen the dagger over the holy water. How could she have done that?

"Priest, do you seek to know my name?" Nicolas whipped his tongue out, like a snake. *"Do you think that will save—"*

Father Prieto swung around. "Frankly, demon, I don't give a shit what your name is." He reached out with the crucifix in his gloved hand, nearly touching Nicholas' head. "In the name of the Lord, I command you to release this boy."

Nicholas shook his head violently. He held up his hands and stepped back. Vomit slid from his lips.

"Dolet, dolet, mammam, dolet," he cried in a high-pitched scream. "Dolet, dolet, mammam, dolet." He repeated the phrase over and over, his body convulsing, head jerking back and forth.

Mary grabbed Father Prieto's arm. Her heart raced; chest ached. She wanted to hold her son. "What is he saying?" she shouted over her son's screams.

Father Prieto kept his hand with the crucifix extended. "It's Latin. He's saying, *it hurts, it hurts, mommy it hurts*."

Mary shook her head. She reached for the crucifix. "Father, stop it."

Father Prieto shoved her back. "We cannot let up. Do not heed his words." His eyes shifted from her to Nicholas. "In the name of Jesus, I command you to leave this boy. In the name of Jesus—"

Nicolas stopped screaming. His convulsions also ceased. He stood silently, glaring at Father Prieto with his black eyes. Finally, his lips parted in a twisted smile, and a wheezy laugh slid from his throat. "Deus tuus non habet potestatem in me," Nicholas uttered. He stepped toward the crucifix, his smile widening.

Father Prieto lowered the cross and backed away. He glanced at Mary. "He says my God has no power over him." He then gazed back at Nicholas. "You're wrong, demon. The Lord has sway over all even creatures of the dark." Father Prieto opened the cap to the bottle he held and flung the clear liquid over Nicholas. "Let His holy water cleanse you from the boy."

The water struck Nicholas across the face and chest, charring his flesh. Black smoke rose from his sizzling skin.

Mary buried her head in her hands. She unleashed a terrible shriek. The stench of her son's smoldering skin was more than she could take. "Stop it… stop it! God make it all stop!" Her pleas fell on deaf ears.

"Does it hurt, demon?" Father Prieto flung more of the liquid, the holy water splashing across Nicholas' stomach and legs, blackening his skin, melting his flesh. "Fear the wrath of God and free this boy."

Nicholas cowered toward a corner. He squealed and roared, like a wild animal, thrashing his arms and legs in every direction.

Father Prieto held up the crucifix and crossed toward Nicholas. "You cannot have this boy, demon."

Nicholas gazed up, his lips twisted in agony. *"Mom, it's me, your little boy. Why are you letting him hurt me?"* His voice was gurgled as if he spoke under water.

Mary, down on her knees, crawled toward her son. "Father, it's Nicholas. He's talking to me. You're killing him… you're killing my son." In the darkness, her fingers came across the dagger she purchased. She grasped the handle and climbed to her feet. "Father, I'm begging you to stop."

Father Prieto shook his head. "We mustn't stop," he shouted. "We must rid this world of this dem—"

"I have to save my son." Mary plunged the blade into his side.

"My lady." Father Prieto fell backward, clumsily reaching for the dagger buried in his flesh. He landed against the bed and slumped to the floor. Shallow breaths slid from his lips. He stared at her with wide eyes. "My lady."

Mary dropped to her knees. What had she done? Taking a deep breath, she raised her chin and gazed at her son. *I did what any good mother would do if their child was suffering.* "Nicholas, Mommy is here. I'll not let anyone hurt you."

Laughter erupted from her son. *"You are a good mommy. You'll raise us well."*

Her son climbed to his feet, his burned flesh falling away, revealing healthy skin underneath. Even the gashes sealed themselves. The black eyes remained.

His bald head pulsated with each beat of his heart. He walked toward Father Prieto, chuckling, revealing his jagged teeth. Once he reached him, he bent down, bringing his face within an inch of the Father's. *"Does it hurt, priest?"*

Father Prieto didn't answer. His eyes dimmed. He wheezed out shallow breaths. He tried to extract the blade from his side, but his hand shook and slid from the handle.

Nicholas kissed the top of Father Prieto's head, then grasped his head with both hands. *"Priest, we sense something about you—some darkness inside of you that causes you pain, makes you seek redemption. If you wish, you may confess your sins to us."*

Mary studied Father Prieto's face. Even in the darkness, she could see it was ashen white. His cheeks trembled, and he rapidly blinked his eyes. He coughed and gasped for a breath but didn't speak.

Nicholas kissed him again on the forehead, then backed away. "I fear your time is short now priest. Even now I can hear your heart slowing. Soon, you will meet your God or mine, and you can tell him the story of how I saved the boy, not you or your God."

Mary tilted her head. What did Nicholas mean?

"I told you, priest, how he asked to join with me." Nicholas smiled triumphantly. *"You see, the boy prayed for help because he was bullied. He prayed for some force to help him to be strong. Who came to his help, priest? Your God? No, it was me. I was the answer to his prayers, and now we will unleash our fury on the world."*

Nicholas paused and gazed at Mary. *"And this fine woman who has finally proven her loyalty will be our mother through it all. Oh, how we have desired to know the love of a mother for her child."* Nicholas smiled wide at her. *"Oh, Mommy, we can already sense your love, and it is everything we dreamed."*

Mary lowered her head to her chest. All those times her son had come home and was quiet after school. Why hadn't he told her what was happening? Why didn't he ask for help? How could she not have known? Her eyes shifted from her son to Father Prieto. "My God, I was wrong. Father, I'm sorry."

Nicholas no longer smiled. His eyes bulged. His lips parted in a sneer *"Shut up, Mommy, or I'll be forced to ki—"*

Nicholas reared his head back and screamed. Spasms coursed through his body. His stomach stretched as if he were pregnant. From inside his body, fingers tried to pry apart his skin. A face pushed against his flesh, then a voice called out as if from a distance. "Mom, where are you? Help me, mom. It's so dark here. I'm so scared—so alone."

"My Nicholas." Sobbing, Mary reached for her son.

"He's mine now." The beast that controlled her son shoved her back. Her son's stomach flattened again. Nicholas' true voice grew distant, then vanished. Only the beast spoke now. *"He and I are one now. You have no choice but to be our mommy—forever."*

Mary started to crawl toward her son. "No, Nicholas, come ba—"

Before she could finish that thought, Father Prieto pounced on her back. "This is the only way, my lady."

She tried to shake him off, but two fangs sunk into her neck, piercing the skin and slicing through flesh, driving deeper and deeper. Blood seeped from her body. She could feel him sucking her life away. A sense of cold swept over her body. At the same time, her own warm blood slid down her neck onto her shoulder. She could hear her own breath growing fainter with each heartbeat. Terror and euphoria mixed together in one final rush, then she was little more than an empty vessel.

She slumped to the floor. The last thing she saw was a bit of early morning light through the shudders.

The last thing she heard was Nicholas' furious bellow.

"Mommy… what have you done, priest?" Nicholas cried out.

"What I prayed I wouldn't have to, demon, but you left me no choice." Father Prieto, blood dripping from his fangs, licked his lips. He ripped out the dagger from his side, then turned away from Nicholas and crossed to his satchel. Ripping off his gloves, he held up both hands to Nicholas. revealing the markings of the cross scarred into his palms. "Demon, you were right when you said there was darkness in me. Darkness has been a part of me for centuries. But I am not seeking redemption. God has already granted that to me. No, demon, today I am seeking vengeance."

Father Prieto reached into his satchel and lifted out two crucifixes. Each burned his hands. Despite the pain and the sound of his own skin sizzling, he placed each cross against his chest and crossed to Nicholas. Wings tore through his jacket and priestly shirt, spreading behind him. His mouth stretched wider; fangs lengthened. He bent down to Nicholas. "You want to possess someone so bad, possess me."

Father Prieto scooped Nicholas up in his arms and buried his teeth deep within his neck, drinking in the boy's blood, tainted with the sourness of a demon's foul lifeforce. It was most distasteful, but he was all too familiar with demon blood. This was different though. Before, he was out to kill the demons. This time…. *As I drink this boy's blood, join with me demon—become one with me. Together we will rule this world.*

Father Prieto could feel the demon resist at first, but as he sank his fangs deeper into the boy's neck, drank more of his blood, the demon relented. Better to possess a vampire than to die with the boy.

When he was finished, Father Prieto released Nicholas. The boy fell to the ground and no longer moved. Stepping over the boy, wiping blood from his mouth, he crossed on shaky legs to the door. His body trembled. His head pounded, like an unseen force twisted a vise around his temples. His thoughts were no longer his own.

This body will belong to us for all time now, priest. You will do my bidding.

Father Prieto smashed his fists through the wall. "No, demon, I am still in control."

The demon laughed. *"No, priest, let's see what chaos we can cause in the name of your God. Oh, the fun we will have as a priest and a creature of night. I thirst for blood, priest. Find me some.*"

Father Prieto grabbed the sides of his head. "Sure, demon. Let's go now." Lumbering from the bedroom, he stumbled down the stairs into the living room, then staggered to the front door. Gripping the doorknob, he uttered. "Time to die, demon."

Throwing the door open, he hobbled out into the morning light. The storm clouds had parted, and the early sun rose in the east, its rays streaking across the sky.

"Don't do this," the demon inside pleaded.

"I have walked this world long enough." Father Prieto extended his hands toward the sky. His fingers and palms ignited. Orange flames spread down his arms.

"It burns, priest."

"Do not fear, demon."

"I am afraid."

"Because you lack faith." Father Prieto arched his head back. Flames burst from his chest. "God, I have been your humble servant, working in the shadows as you commanded of me. "I now offer you my spirit."

In a blinding flash, the fire engulfed Father Prieto. He smiled one last time, then burst into ashes.

The demon cried out, *no*, and then was silenced.

***

"Mom, I have a strange thirst."

Mary, her legs weak, insides like an empty cavern, cradled her son in her arms and caressed his blond hair. She gazed into his light blue eyes and smiled. "I know, Nicholas, I have the same thirst." The craving for blood was almost maddening, but she forced herself to remain calm for her son. What the hell had Father Prieto done to them?

She peered through Nicholas' bedroom window. Night had once again fallen. They were safe for the moment but what would happen at daybreak? How could he have done this to them? He'd taken away one curse and left them both with another. What kind of life could Nicholas have now? "God, what have we become?" she whispered.

She lifted Nicholas and carried him to his bed, gently laying him down. At least he had no memory of the demon, no memory of how his father died and no memory of Father Prieto. He was Nicholas again—but not really.

"But Mom, I'm not tired." He sat up in his bed. "I'm just so thirsty."

Mary ran her tongue over her fangs. There was only one way to satisfy their thirst. She again peered through the curtain. Some poor victim's blood awaited them. God, I don't want to be a killer, but what choice do I hav—?"

Her eyes focused on Father Prieto's satchel on the nightstand. She lifted it up and peered inside. "Oh my." Her heart raced. She took a deep breath. She reached in and removed several bags filled with blood.

She also spied a white envelope.

Opening it, she found a letter from Father Prieto, one he must have written even before he crossed into her home.

Tears slid down her cheeks as she read it.

"My lady, if you are reading this, then that means I made an unfair choice, and you probably feel like I have condemned you and your son to a fate worse than death. I imagine I have also passed on as well in a final sacrifice that I made happily. I can only say that I wish there had been some other way, but I sensed it was too late even before I arrived at your doorstep, and I knew I would face a terrible choice. I supposed I could have killed your son and the demon, but I wanted to provide

him and you a chance to live again. So, yes, I transitioned him. And I knew he would need you more than ever, so I did the same to you. I want you to know what you do now is completely your choice. You can choose to be a monster, or you can become something else. You do not need to kill to survive. There are other ways, and the Holy Father can help. You will find his direct phone number below. Just remember what I told you.... Do not fear the dark. It is not the enemy of light. My lady, even we vampires have a place in this world and in the next."

There was a break in the writing followed by a telephone number.

Mary looked up from the letter toward the bags of blood. A slight smile crossed her face. "Nicholas, honey, time to feed."

CADAVARS IN CONVERSATION

Rob Tucker

They didn't even keep my original name.

I knew there must be some way I could get back.

My real panic was hearing the doctor pronounce me brain dead. I couldn't respond and tell him NO! Even though I was shouting, he and the attendant nurses didn't hear me.

Then I was carted off to the morgue and prepared for transference to the medical school. Even the embalming process didn't stop my mind from working. I began to think maybe this wasn't my mind fighting to find my way back to life, but something else, some manifestation of myself that wouldn't move on.

Donating myself as a cadaver was less costly than a funeral or other options. Even cremation turned out to be costly, as well as contaminating the air from the extreme heat of the furnace.

I had always believed death was endless darkness without cognition. But here I was supposed to have died, and I was still thinking, trying to find a way to get back. I was convinced I could do it. I just had to find the portal or whatever it was that could make my return happen.

Then I thought perhaps I was more intensely remembering my family and friends than they remembered me. I didn't want to be a restless spirit but I thought that was better than non-existence in endless night. I quickly realized I possessed little if any spiritual control. I could not direct myself to do anything. I was at the mercy of memories. So, I assumed memory might be my portal back to life.

I discovered I couldn't remember what I wanted to. There was no structure or cohesion, only surreal dream-like distortions. I wasn't inside my head and body anymore. Some substance of my former self I couldn't describe roiled outside.

I could look back and see the embalmed exoskeleton of my dead former self but I was no longer inside and had no way of getting back inside and reanimating myself.

I snatched the first impression I could latch onto and retain as a starting point. It wasn't anything I could see, only hear. Someone was playing the piano, a piece composed by Beethoven. I couldn't place it at first. Maintaining a sense of focus was difficult. I was trying to reconcile myself being not dead when I was in fact dead.

I tried to move toward the sound with no reference to time and space and could not pinpoint the location of its source. If I could not even make the player of the piano piece materialize, how could I possibly bring myself back to life?

Sound. The piano was sound. Although limited and restricted to one kind of sound, it was one of my senses. My senses had to be a clue to my returning. In the void of endless darkness, I went in search of memory fragments and impressions related to my other senses. They just weren't coming to me. I couldn't find them. I drifted in an aimless search.

The movement of a shapeless shadow caught my attention. I moved toward it hoping it would materialize into a memory.

"Who are you?" I asked. "I thought I was in here alone."

"You're not. I was here before you. See those other dissection tables? There are eight of us here."

"How long have you been here?"

"Two years. Probably won't be here much longer. I'm pretty well carved up."

"Two years? How did you get here?"

"The same way you did."

"I don't remember."

"It's just as well."

"Two years. How could you stand it?"

"Not that I had a choice."

"Did they give you another name?"

"Just shortened it from Carlotta to Carol. But the anatomy students prefer not to give us names. They don't actually get to know anything personal about us until they finish the class after one year."

"Maybe they did the same to my name."

"What was it?"

"Andrew. The student team working on me call me Andy. They're a nice group. Six of them. Three young men and three women. They're grateful. They treat me with respect."

"Not a big deal."

"It is a big deal. I thought being dead was being dead."

"Kaput."

"Yeah, kaput. I shouldn't be able to talk to you or however we're communicating. We're not sentient anymore. We're just cadavers preserved in formaldehyde."

Carol laughed.

"It's not a laughing matter."

"Think of our body bags as a health spa wrap."

"Health spa?" I laughed. "Are you crazy?"

"It's important to keep a sense of perspective."

"We only see each other as cadavers."

"Actually, we're spirits."

"Do you hover over the student team and observe them peeling away your skin and fatty tissue and cutting into your muscle and bone?"

"Of course, what else is there to do? Besides, I'm learning more about my body parts than I knew before I died."

"What did you die from?"

"Brain cancer. You?"

"Heart attack and stroke," I said. "Brought on by diabetes."

"Both? Bummer."

"Well, I brought it on myself. Over-indulged so I was told. But hell, when you're in your eighties, you should be able to indulge and enjoy the things you like. What's the point not? Unless you're trying to live to be one hundred."

"I am one hundred," said a voice from another cadaver two tables down from mine. "I should say I died at one hundred, two months after my birthday."

"You really were an old fart," said Carol.

"We're all old farts."

"You can't accuse me of being an old fart."

"I'm not accusing you. Just stating the obvious."

"I did not die old. I was young by your standard."

"How old were you?"

"I won't say but I was a little more than half your age."

"Damn, you were still a hot tomato."

"Watch yourself. I don't take kindly to misogynistic insults."

"Calling a young woman a hot tomato is not an insult. It's a compliment."

"You're just one of those white-haired old men who never learned any better. You're prejudiced against women."

"The hell I am. I loved women. I loved my wife when she was alive. She died ten years before me."

"Speaking of prejudice," I interrupted, "my wife insisted I had to wear a collared shirt and not a T-shirt when I went out in public."

"What's prejudiced about that? That's just good taste and common sense."

"It's prejudice. She said being old that I should wear a collared shirt."

"Good for her. Maybe you can recreate me as your memory of her. Say my name and hold me in your memory. Time is running out. I am drifting into endless night."

"Oh, don't be so melodramatic. As being dead goes, our situation isn't so bad. It could be worse."

"What do you mean worse?"

"If we had been cremated or decomposed into mulch, our spirits would have been destroyed. Only cadavers have spirits that survive death."

"Well, at least that's something."

"All that religious mythology about floating around in heaven is nonsense," I said.

"People did talk about that when I was dying."

"It just makes them feel better about the unknown. More secure."

"Well, at least you and I know."

"I think it would have been better to be mulched or cremated. Being the spirit of a cadaver is boring."

"How so? How do you feel anything?"

"Oh, I have feelings. Strong emotions. So do you actually."

"I can't say that I do."

"You aren't tenderized enough. Give the formaldehyde a few days. Once a medical student starts working on you, life can get interesting."

"Life? We're cadavers. We don't have life."

"We are a bridge between life and death for the students who dissect us."

"Never thought of myself that way."

"Stick with me, Babe. I'm the voice of experience. Think of me as your mentor."

"There's nothing left for me to learn."

"There are all kinds of things for you to explore."

"Like what?"

"We can have an affair."

I laughed. "That's impossible. We're not sentient. We're not alive. And think what would happen if a medical student discovered our cadavers having sex."

"We use our imagination, Andy. We use our imagination."

"How can you possibly feel erotic?"

"I have memories," she said. "I do have memories."

"You do? How did you find them? I've been trying without success."

"Your memories really don't matter. You can't do anything about anything anymore anyway."

"I murdered my wife."

"You what?"

"I murdered my wife."

"You're bullshitting me. I don't believe you."

"But I did. I actually did."

"Then you're just the one I've been looking for."

"Looking for?"

"Yes, as a partner in crime and murder."

"Well, I didn't actually murder her."

"But you did kill her in some way, right?"

"Not really physically. I loved her too much."

"Come on, out with it. Tell me the truth. What did you do? What happened?"

"I just thought you might be impressed if I told you that."

"Why do you want to impress me?"

"We're just floating around here in limbo. I thought the subject might be interesting to alleviate the boredom of waiting."

"Why did you say that?"

"I thought I might impress you."

"Impress me. You're weird. Why would you want to impress me?"

"Now that we're released from our bodies, we could be partners."

"You mean agents of death."

"Oh – HA HA HA! What makes you think we're agents of death?"

"Well, because we died. Now we can fly around and make the spirits of other dead people join up with us. You know. We could all party."

"That sounds sick but I like it. I need some purpose in limbo. I need to flex my vibrations."

"Or, we could invade people's minds with good moral and ethical thoughts."

"Doesn't sound very exciting. Sounds boring. I like your first suggestion."

"Do you know where it originated?"

"No, where?"

"I murdered my husband."

"I don't believe you. You're just saying that because I told you I murdered my wife, and I admitted I didn't."

"Did she die before you?"

"No, I died first."

"Then she's still alive."

"Yes, and in relatively good health."

"Nobody our age is in relatively good health. If they are, they won't be for long. There's an end to life for all of us."

"Okay, I'll give you that. Here we are. You and I are at the end and still talking to each other. And you want to party. We shouldn't even exist."

"We don't. We're only spirits having a chat before..."

"Before what?"

"Before we move on."

"Move on to what?"

"Nothingness. Endless darkness. Our existence is in the memories of those who are still alive who we left behind."

"I wonder what they remember?"

"Depends on who you were as a live person. Good, bad, or a combination of something in-between."

"Are you just making all this up? You don't know any more than I do."

"So we have to wait until we find out and then what we learn won't matter. We'll have no way to deal with it, no choice in the matter."

"Well, that's not very positive."

"There's nothing positive about dying except that your body is too old and worn out to keep you alive."

"I was in pretty good shape for my age. But you know. So what are we going to do next?"

"Since your wife is still alive, how about we haunt her?"

"How can we do that? We're spirits, not ghosts."

"Same thing."

"Not really. I mean how do spirits in our condition haunt someone or anything?"

"Through their memory. You said our existence is in the memories of those who are still alive who we left behind. So, we invade her memory of you."

"That's not possible."

"Anything's possible. You just have to believe something, and it will happen."

"Then I'd like to believe I'm still alive."

"Except for that. We can't change being dead."

"For a minute there, I thought you were on to something. I was trying to remember her and my life before, but I didn't have any way to get there."

"You have to find yourself in her memories of you."

"That's not haunting. You call that haunting?"

"Well, we spirits do have limitations."

"Okay, how do I get into her memories of me?"

"You can't."

"Why are you doing this to me?"

"I'm going to leave you now."

"What is this? What is happening? You can't leave me now. You said we could haunt her."

"Sorry about that. You said you just wanted something to occupy you while you are waiting."

"But how will I know what she remembers about me?"

"Very soon, that won't matter to you."

"What do you mean? I thought we were going to have a good time, a party. You said you wanted to have a party."

"I created an illusion for you."

"What good does that do me?"

"Follow me and you will find out."

"Follow you where?"

"Into endless darkness."

"But I don't want to go there."

"You don't have any choice."

"Who are you anyway?"

"I am your death angel."

"If you are an angel, there is supposed to be a heaven, and endless darkness doesn't sound like heaven to me."

"You don't understand death, but you expect to understand heaven? Besides, did I say I was taking you to heaven?"

"You're not an angel, are you?"

"Saying I'm the angel of death seems to be more calming to my charges than calling myself the Grim Reaper."

"I'm not going to heaven, am I?"

"Let's find out, shall we?"

The students gathered near the cadaver gasped at the sudden unexplained whoosh of chill air that fogged their goggles and fluttered what little hair escaped their disposable bouffant hats. They looked around in confusion, then at each other.

"That wasn't creepy at all," the science intern said.

"Just think. You're going to be working in your family's mortuary, so you'll get to witness the comings and goings of the dead on a daily basis," one of the med students said. They all laughed, relieving the tension before they got back to work.

THE END OF THE LINE - CHAPTER 1

Francesca Quarto

"Thanks for not trampling my little girl while you shoved past us!"

The woman was pissed and there was no time to explain that I was on a life and death mission. Yeah, I know that sounds corny, but it was true. A life hung by a thread and that thread was shredding with every second.

She continued to rant to the folks standing in the jittery line behind her. The checkout girl began to ring up the four steaks.

"Seriously! Is your barbeque so important that you cut ahead of other people instead of going to the end of the line like a civilized person?"

The irate mother continued to scold me, her voice louder and attracting unwanted attention. I nervously looked out the large glass window watching the dark gather in scattered pools outside the reach of the parking lot lights. Now, other voices joined the righteous tirade, sounding like her backup singers. The little blond-headed girl I was accused of nearly trampling whimpered something about not liking the lady with the green monster on her t-shirt. I figured she'd never seen a Godzilla movie. She said I was scary in a four-year-olds unmodulated voice. Everyone in both check-out lines were now eyeing me like I'd sprouted devil horns. I began to feel sweat gather under my arms and run down my sides.

Will this woman ever finish! I thought frantically. The clerk was turning the largest package of meat over and over searching for the bar code as if it moved like ants on a dead bird.

I heard her mumble, "Some folks must have a whole lot of money."

I cleared my throat loudly, sighing when the cash register dinged and the drawer slid open. I handed the girl my hundred-dollar bill. I'd been saving it in case of extreme emergency and this qualified!

"Oh, gee. I have to have my manager check anything that big. I'll page him. Shouldn't take a minute. Ralph Pines come to register three please. Ralph to register three."

I stopped myself from reaching across and throttling her scrawny neck, but the other customers had a good description of me by now so I resisted. Two minutes later the manager was holding my hundred up to the light and finally pronounced it legal tender. I grabbed my bag of meat and turned to the mother still muttering her displeasure. She moved the little girl behind her protectively.

"There is a five-dollar bill near your foot," I said and turned toward the door. I figured her wait was worth that.

I'd parked my car in a shadowy alley across the street from the grocery store. I spotted a gray shape in the front seat. It was hunched over as if reading, or in this case, dying. I hurried, scurrying like a rat away from the light and toward the comfort of the shadows.

The alley was empty except for my twice-handed-down Beatle. Being the youngest of three girls I was usually the beneficiary of every out-grown piece of clothing, or in this case, a vintage Volkswagen. Somehow, I recently managed to graduate from St. Felicita Academy. The good sisters were probably glad to see the last of me as much as I was to escape their scrutiny and narrowing of eyes at my un-lady-like behavior. Leaving that all behind, summer days spread out hot and lazy, like the warm sands and lulling waves of the Key West shore. I was in day four of three glorious weeks with my best friends, Jamie and Liz, and my recue dog, Harry. We pooled our graduation money and rented a bungalow near the ocean. I begged off the third party on the beach that night so I could hang with Harry and catch up on some spectacular star gazing.

I'd been hooked as a young child on studying the stars and the myriads of astral bodies floating just out of reach of our imagination. Being over-confident rather than an over-achiever, I knew this was my calling. I would reach the stars one way or another.

I got a lot of flak from the others for packing my beautiful graduation gift; a light-weight Stargazer-300 with easy-carry tripod. Guess they suspected I'd choose the celestial bodies over the muscled beach bodies they were drooling over. Grabbing my gear and Harry's leash I headed for the higher sand dunes outlined against a night sky, shimmering in the fractured light of a trillion stars.

Harry slowed my progress, sniffing, peeing, and trying to catch the sand crabs that seemed to cover the wet beach one second and vanish the next. We climbed to the top of a steep dune, high and clear of any obstacles. After filling Harry's portable bowl with water from my backpack, I set up the tripod and carefully attached the telescope. Adjusting the scope to a comfortable height and angle I began my visual journey through endless space.

The hours passed as if attached to a comet's tail. The full moon shifting in its determined progress, hung overhead. I studied its craters, wishing I had been with the astronauts that walked upon its craggy surface so long ago. The rhythm of the waves, seagulls calling as they scoured for food along the darkened shoreline, were the only sounds as I found the stars and planets spinning in their unique orbits above me. As always, I mentally shrank to insignificance, mesmerized by this earthbound view of the heavens.

I was lost in Jupiter's rings when Harry jumped to his feet, breaking my concentration. Before I could react, he took off down the dune throwing sand in his wake as he headed to the water's edge. By the time I got there, he was soaked, running into the smaller waves lapping at the shore's edge. He was very agitated, and I grabbed his collar, but as I looked out at the rolling water, I understood why.

A silver object bobbed among the white caps crowning the stronger rollers, moving with the waves like a surfboard without the surfer. I watched as a huge wave gathered in the distance. The object was pulled back as the wave rose like a monster from the depths.

The silver form glinted back to the moon an SOS as it lifted higher on the crest. A minute later it was dragged under as the wave curled over it like a black hand. I stood frozen; my feet unsteady in the shifting sand until the mysterious object came rushing into shore with the power of the water's surge. Harry went bonkers and we both got soaked. I worried about losing him to the rushing waters undertow, moving us backward as quickly as the grasping sand would allow.

The strange object was coming in with such force it plowed like a steam shovel into the dune behind us. Harry was strangely quiet, his tail up and his eyes fixed on the object embedded in the warm sand.

Looking over what was exposed from a safe distance, my initial reaction was this could be a part from a rocket launched from Cape Canaveral. It appeared to be a fairly long cylindrical object though a good portion was buried. I circled the lodged tubular mystery. There was no obvious seam indicating how it could be opened, and no visible markings. Engrossed with the possibilities my excitable mind conjured, I let go of Harry's collar. He immediately began digging into the wet sand covering the rest of the cylinder. I knelt down and started scooping away the heavy sand until more of the silver tube was exposed and my fingers were nearly raw.

The moon shifted overhead like an unblinking Cyclops eye, watching us as we shifted the sand. Harry was panting, flopping down with his head on a paw. I knelt back on my heels, too tired to do more than take in more of the exposed container. I was certain there was something remarkable inside its slivery walls but wasn't prepared when the top of the cylinder flew back with the sound of a large exhale full of strange odors. A rasping sound, like sandpaper over wood, floated up from the capsule's interior. Harry moved to my side taking a protective stance.

We both stood transfixed when a starkly white hand curled six long, knobby digits around the curve of the outer wall. I blinked and backed away. Harry followed suit, less sure of his protective role. A second hand quickly appeared, followed by more rasping sounds. Whatever was inside the silver capsule was taking its sweet time getting out. My curiosity overcame my fear as I approached the cylinder.

THE END OF THE LINE - CHAPTER 2

Francesca Quarto

Two disk-shaped eyes looked up at me, the creamy moonlight swimming in their inky depths. I jerked back, surprised and more than a little afraid of confronting aliens from inside the beached capsule. Harry whined softly, glued to my leg I could feel him quivering. We watched a slender, chalky-white figure begin to rise from the murky depths of the capsule and leapt out onto the sand. It was naked but had no physical traits of any gender that I was familiar with. From its small stature I thought it was a child. It swayed slightly on spindly legs. I took another step back when I saw they ended in splayed feet like some kind of bird, three toes on each foot, tipped in sharp-looking curved nails. Now that it was fully illuminated by the bright moon, I could see the creature's body was as translucent as a jellyfish, with the same gelatinous look as it began to move toward me.

I was about to run when a high voice held me like a strong magnet.

"I pose no threat to you or your companion. My mission here is nearly complete and I am already in transition for lack of nourishment…or…in your language…I will soon die."

The being, whatever it was, definitely was not of this world. I heard the word *die* and it triggered a very alarmed human response.

"Do you mean you're dying…like dead…right here in front of me?"

A long gurgle came from the creature's lipless mouth. It immediately grabbed hold of the side of the strange capsule as if he was exhausted by our conversation.

"My apologies for finding humor in your comment. I have long studied your species and find much of your understanding of events laughable in its naïveté. But you are still in the tender stage of your evolutionary cycle. I must explain so much more, and yet, my own cycle will close if I don't find sustenance within three hours of your time construct."

"Are there others like you that could help you now? I have no idea what you need to eat."

"I am alone on this assignment. No others will come as this task was given me by the Council of Originators. As for what I must have to survive long enough to see my orders through the end, we are carnivores as much of your kind. Though there are no Runkle beasts on this insignificant planet, my ship's enviro-species sensor was able to identify a similar food source you named 'cow.' This will sustain my strength until my mission is completed."

I thought over this odd comment about cows and almost laughed when the visitor asked that I secure a cow saying, "I will render it ready to devour."

I said there was no way I could find a cow in the seaside town, but I would go to a grocery store and buy some steaks.

"Are these 'steaks' from the same creature?"

I assured the being they were, asking if there was some way to hide the transporter, preferably with him inside. I realized I had begun to think of the being as male. So, I asked if he was the male or female of his kind and what his name was.

"There are no such gender designations needed. We are one. You may use my coda, Chirta. If you wish to continue questioning me in this trivial manner, however, you must secure the cow flesh, or my expiration will be inevitable by the time your moon is lost to the rise of your one sun."

Thirty minutes later, back in the car, I was glad we decided that Chirta should ride along so he could begin eating the steaks immediately. Even in the deeply shadowed alley I felt twitchy, sure some permanent resident would run across my car and be curious enough to check it out. Numbers of young tourists had already come to the attention of the local sheriff's department and warnings issued. My visitor wore my hoodie, with a beach towel covering his glow-in-the-dark white legs. His hunched manner of sitting with his legs drawn up to his chest made me feel like I was riding with a giant toad beside me in my tiny car.

The three steaks proved short work for the slender figure. I watched wide-eyed as a long purplish tongue flicked out to lick a bloody trail off his fingers. Chirta caught my expression which likely showed some disgust at his eating manners.

"There is no need to judge how I feed myself human. Your own kind have nearly destroyed your oceans with poisons, devouring the denizens of the waters to near extinction."

My first reaction was to argue, then I realized he had a point.

"Let's get back to your transporter, Chirta, before someone gets curious about my car."

We drove as close to the dunes as possible without getting stuck and hiked to the tall sand hill where the capsule was mostly buried, only the silvery nose poking out. The moonlight was more vapor than solid now as thick clouds scudded across its face.   Chirta immediately stepped back into his craft, reemerging holding a small implement studded with various blinking colored light. He pressed one yellow button and I watched open-mouthed as the heavy sand covering the capsule lifted like a blanket, floating several feet away before dropping to form a smooth mound. Having only a brief look earlier, I was struck by the unusual appearance of the capsule.

"It's…it looks like a rocket or missile," I said, walking around the sleek transporter.

"It's merely an exploration unit, designed to enter alien planets without detection."

"Alien? Wow, that's rich! I hate to point out that *you're* the alien here, Chirta."

He ignored the logic in my comment and fiddled with the small tool. As I watched, he pushed various buttons that brightened and dimmed like Christmas lights. Looking at me with lidless onyx eyes, he told me he had something to show me inside his 'intergalactic grazer' as he called his transporter. I got an immediate chill of apprehension. Did I really want to be inside the strange vehicle with a ghostly pale creature from another world?

Before I had to answer that question, Harry sidled up to me, a low moan making me step back from the star grazer. Did he sense something dangerous inside the darkness?

Chirta took a small step toward me and Harry moved in front of me. I'd never seen Harry act so aggressively, but then I'd never been holding conversations with an alien life form either. Chirta raised his long, boney hand and pointed to the object he used to scoop away the sand directly at Harry. Harry's yelp of surprise echoed mine when he was lifted off his paws and dropped like a discarded stuffed toy into the inky interior of the grazer.

THE END OF THE LINE - CHAPTER 3

Francesca Quarto

I think I screamed out Harry's name before the same instrument was pointed in my direction. Suddenly, I hung like a bird caught in a cross wind and dropped unceremoniously into the capsule. I felt Harry's fur against my leg and heard his whimper of distress. I had no time to react to being kidnapped by Chirta because everything happened so quickly. There was a thump and more darkness as the ship's top was secured, a sucking vacuum sound ensuring its travel worthiness. Lights began to flash all around us, making me blink furiously with the sudden brightness. Chirta moved silently, passing fingers over instrument panels. A soft hum began to fill the silence of the cabin. I knew we'd be lifting off the beach and shooting into the night sky within a few breaths.

"Wait! I don't think kidnapping me is the best way to show your gratitude for me saving your life! I could have let you starve to death, remember?"

"Have you not been studying the mantle that covers your earth in your limited fashion? I am saving you from inevitable termination. You will be carefully tended to as we evaluate you along with the other earth seedlings we've harvested throughout your brief existence. Many were planted after the great planet-killer destroyed most life on your world. Earthlings have been scattered throughout the galaxies we travel to determine on which home planet they will likely thrive. You are the last of your species to be culled from this dying planet for now. Your kind has failed miserably in heeding warnings and testimonies over the eons of how your destructive behavior has polluted the very air you breathe to survive. Our experiment here has failed and so we have chosen a random selection of humans to start over on the many worlds we visit. We must wait and see how they fair, but our cycles of life are nearly endless so there is no hurry."

When Chirta turned away to fuss over the panel of glowing lights, I felt a cold knot settle in my stomach. How could this be happening? I huddled close to Harry and tried to fathom Chirta's words; we humans were no more than planted seeds upon the face of our planet. A garden of vast proportions, covering the continents with our species, dominating all other life forms. I guess we've grown wild, left untended by the Gardener. Now, there will be a reckoning and Earth will be a dying planet among the galaxies unless my kidnapper and his kind find some value in our survival and intervene. Maybe my small kindness in saving his life will induce a similar generosity on his part when Chirta returns us to his home planet. Maybe Harry and I will live to see another day on another world.

The darkness closed around the speeding ship like a fist. Harry's whimpers receded into the blackness as my thoughts became a jumble of fear, excitement and a desperate sadness, aware I'd never see my family again. But there was that kernel of exhilaration. Other worlds, other species, questions answered! What had I really left behind? Yes, my family, but I could remember them all as they were when I left and not be witness to their decline or human suffering. I was forced to make a trade; forced against my will if truth be told. But sitting in the dull glow from the throbbing lights on the dashboard of this vehicle, I knew my world had just expanded like a balloon and I just prayed it wouldn't burst.

Chirta looked down at me pressed against the silvery wall of the compartment.

"You're entering a different ecosphere human. My kind honor the Great Designer of all that is, and we are incapable of harming any sentient life. Unlike your species, who slaughter any and all living creatures indiscriminately. If all goes well, you will be returned to teach your world the truths and lessons you witness on my planet. Perhaps."

I felt Harry shift slightly as he got to his feet. As if called to his side, he padded over to where Chirta stood at the console. I became alarmed when I saw Chirta held the small object he used on Harry and me earlier. He pointed it at Harry. I screamed "No!" struggling to get up, my legs numb from being curled under me for…how long?   I swayed unsteadily, reaching for Harry's collar. I heard the low hum coming from the mechanism and knew it was too late. Harry was gone. In his place stood a replica of Chirta who was welcoming him with strange clicks and low gurgling sounds.

"Do not be concerned human," Chirta was saying as I collapsed to my knees.

"This is Baxt, placed in your world as a foundling to be brought into your home. Baxt has been with you for many of your year cycles and will be with you always as your companion."

I looked up from the floor of the ship and thought back to the many nights Harry slept at the foot of my bed at home, licked my face with loving kisses, and followed me like a faithful guardian angel. I was unaware of the tears wetting my face until Baxt stretched out his pale arm, gently wiping my check. Leaning into the curve of the wall I realized I felt calm and unafraid. Harry wasn't really gone; he was never here. A random thought infiltrated my drifting mind. Were there others on Earth, in our world, in *my* world? Other aliens taking forms we knew and even loved. The Gardeners have been here all along and have only shown themselves when Earthlings reached the end of the line. When our world was in the throes of upheaval and distress.

I closed my eyes and felt Baxt sit beside me. I reached over, my eyes still closed and found his bony hand, letting the long fingers wrap around mine.

HATCHED

Rob Tucker

I'm luxuriating in a warm bath in a transparent flower vase that gives me the appearance of being a fetus on display floating in a laboratory jar. But I'm not in a laboratory. I'm in the modern kitchen of a family in a residential suburb.

I attribute my good fortune to the discovery and research by a toy manufacturer of a new prehistoric substance that has allowed me to hatch from its egg-like properties. I don't think the toy manufacturer fully knows what he has stumbled upon but that's okay. I do. It's my secret until I choose to reveal it. My reality must be realized by those who purchased me, and they must come to love me as one of their own.

During my gestation, my head and limbs and tail unfolded from the soft pink sponge-like mass of my egg that expanded by absorbing the water in which I was submerged.

What I learned from watching and listening to the adults and children could fill volumes but I am an impatient fellow and anxious to get on with my evolutionary life as a member of the human family. I want to be the family pet.

The two boys called me Pinky.

With a name like Pinky, who would ever take me seriously? I'm a genuine dinosaur with vast intelligence accumulated over a gazillion years. I should have a name like Tronasaur or Megasaur that identifies me as a powerful prehistoric beast. There is literally no imagination in the name Pinky. It affects and influences adult humans in a negative way, so they don't believe I'm real and, worst of all, they don't take me seriously. I would have to teach them a lesson.

In the first place, their diet was unsatisfactory for me. They ate cooked meat and vegetables of which all were unappetizing. I was not a vegetarian. I was a carnivore. I had to have raw live meat as a sustainable diet to perpetuate the evolutionary forces within me. Why would humans ruin perfectly good raw live meat by cooking it? They slaughtered it but that took half the enjoyment away for me. The cries and shrieks and squeaks and squawks and squeals were essential to my *mise en place* since their noises of distress were expressions of love for me. Dinosaur love is a special kind of love.

Once I ingested a raw creature, it became compressed within my soft pink prehistoric substance to be carried forward with me into the future. I was an agent of evolution. Therefore, I didn't reveal myself to be included at the dinner table. I just observed the parents and children and felt great sympathy over the pleasures they were depriving themselves. I finally accepted they were behind in the evolutionary process.

The boys took me out of my environmental bath and played with me as a toy. They talked and interacted with me as a real entity. We shared existential happiness through their imagination.

Problems started to arise, no pun intended, when I felt the urge to find a mate. At a certain point in their lives, all male dinosaurs needed a mate to take care of their urges.

What the adults didn't know about me was that I could emerge from my vase and metamorphose into a full-size dinosaur, something I only did secretly during the night. Since my body material was soft and pliable, I could manipulate a lock and slip out through a partially open door.

I knew there had to be more of my kind. At night, I went out in search for siblings and relatives and lonely female dinosaurs. I was a strapping male with a strong drive to propagate and perpetuate our evolutionary species and convert the X gene that prevented humans from rejoining us as the dominate intelligent life form.

The late-night dog walkers and free roaming cats and small wild animals were easy pickings. Nobody heard their screams, and they didn't wake anybody. I was well-nourished.

Large pink piles of my turds in public parks and on neighborhood lawns confounded forensic analysis by the city and county pest and vector control departments. My turds became a breaking wind news item associated with missing dogs and their human walkers. In my miniature form in my containment bottle, I saw news anchors and pundits discussing their existence on the family television.

Then one night when I was out roaming a wooded park in search of a meal, my world changed. Terry (another tyrannosaurus) was a hot pink hottie. Once she batted her long eyelashes at me, I was a goner. Owned by children in a family across town, she told me she also transformed from a miniature toy like me to a full-grown dinosaur. I started thinking of the possibility that, depending on how many of us existed as toys, as a species, we might repopulate the earth.

We decided that now that we had found each other, we did not want to return to our miniature selves. The time had come to declare our true existence and claim our place in the modern world. To our dismay, the modern world feared us and didn't want us. All people had to do was feed us live humans and animals to keep us happy. We meant them no harm.

Police cars with screaming sirens chased us and helicopters flew overhead tracking us as we ran along city streets. Our giant feet crunched cars and trucks and flattened people trying to scramble out of the way.

I didn't know why the mob of outraged humans screamed and shouted and shook their fists at us. They even tried to shoot us, but their bullets just bounced off our impenetrable pink hides. So, we went on the run as fugitives out onto vast deserts and hid in remote mountains.

Somehow, Terry and I would have to convince humans to love and accept us. We thought having a baby dinosaur or two and raising a family like humans with our own different needs and cultural values would do the trick. But that would have to be a future undertaking.

Human evolution was so far behind. Why did evolutionary conversion have to be so difficult?

THE SLASHER'S REMORSE

Darren Simon

Billy stood over his latest victim, blood dripping from his gloves and the curved dagger he'd used to rip out her insides one organ at a time. Flayed from her chest down to her stomach, he marveled at the human body when revealed for the glorious artwork it truly was. Bending down closer, he listened as she gasped one final whimper, one last breath, then was silent. A last tear streaked down her cheek. Her mouth remained twisted in her final expression of terror.

She never saw his face underneath his mask, but if she had, she would know how much joy she'd brought him by the wide smile he couldn't suppress. His entire body tingled, just like it always did.

Reaching into her chest, prying apart her bones until they cracked, he tore out her heart. Holding it to his nose, the salty, meaty odor made his mouth water. Saliva dripped from between his lips, down his chin and neck.

His body shivered. He couldn't wait any longer. He bit into her heart and swooned over the gush of blood that filled his mouth. He drank it down and then bowed to her—a quiet thank you for the gift she'd given him.

He gazed at her one more time. He didn't know her—didn't need to know her. She was just another victim this night. She couldn't have been much older than twenty-five. She had been lovely before with long blond hair and porcelain skin, but now she was perfect.

"Onto the next." He bowed to her one more time. "The night is you—"

"Billy, what have you done?"

Billy's insides froze. Even in the darkened office, he knew who the voice belonged to. "Doctor Leyana," he uttered.

He turned toward the office door, and there she stood, hand over her mouth, blue eyes bulging.

"My God, Billy." She shook her head and shielded her eyes with her hands.

His gaze shifted from Doctor Leyana to his victim and then back to his psychiatrist. *Oh, dear God. I'm a monster.* His pulse quickened. He suddenly felt hollow inside. How could he have let this happen? How could he let the beast out again? "I'm sorry, Doc. What are you doing here? How'd you find me?"

Doctor Leyana hung her head, her curly red hair covering her face. "Billy, don't you remember? You called me asking for help. I told you to stay home… that I'd come see you, but you were gone, so I tracked your phone—here. Oh, Billy."

She turned to leave the office.

"No, don't go." He crossed toward her.

"Stay back," she screamed.

He slid to a stop. Realizing he still had the bloody dagger in his gloved hand, he let it slip through his fingers to the floor. "It's all right, Doc. Look, I let go of the blade. You know I would never hurt you. All you've ever done is try to help me." He dropped to his knees and started to sob. "I'm sick, Doc. I'm so sick. I've blown everything we've worked so hard for."

"Billy, how many more have you killed tonight?" Doctor Leyana's voice cracked.

He held up his hands and sobbed louder. "I… I don't know. I couldn't help myself. I wanted so much to turn them into art. I wanted to taste their flesh. I tried to control it. I tried so hard, but I couldn't—"

Doctor Leyana backed toward the door. Even in the darkness, he could see her hands shaking. "Billy, you have to turn yourself in."

He lunged at her, wrapping his arms around her waist, blood from his victim staining her white business skirt. He pressed his head against her smooth black silk blouse. He squeezed her tightly and felt her quiver. "Doc, no, you have to help me. I'm afraid. You're the only one I can trust. You've always been the only one. I know you can make me better again—just like before."

She tried to break his grip. "Billy, please… don't hurt me. I don't want to die."

A spark of rage made his insides boil. He slowly stood up until he towered over her, then grasped the sides of her head with hands so large they nearly covered her face. He locked eyes with her. She trembled. Tears slid down her cheeks. "How could you say that to me, Doc? I could never hurt you. You're not like the others. You're special to me, and I know I'm special to you. Tell me I'm special to you." He shook her face harder than he meant to.

She nodded. "Y… yes, Billy, you are special to me."

Sweat poured from his face, plastering his mask to his skin. "Are you lying to me?"

"No, never." Doctor Leyana stopped shivering. She blinked away her tears. She placed her small, dainty hands over his and then held them, like a mother comforting a child. "You always were special to me."

He dropped to his knees again. "Then you'll help me?" He leaned forward and kissed her hands. Doc was his only hope. She had helped him control the beast within before. She could do it again.

Doctor Leyana offered a gentle smile. It was a source of comfort even in the darkness. "Billy, I will help you, but you have to do two things for me, and they won't be easy." Her voice was steadier.

"I'll do whatever you want." Billy retreated a couple of steps. "Just make the nightmare go away. Rid me of the beast within for good."

She crossed to him and reached up to his face with one hand. "I need you to remove your mask. I need to see the real you."

Billy shook his head. "I... I can't."

"Billy, you must."

He closed his eyes and balled his hands into fists. His mind screamed *no* in silence, but Doc was right. Shivering, he lifted his hands to his mask and slowly removed it. Once in his hands, he held it before his eyes. Oh, it was so beautiful. The cadaver skin had been the perfect canvas for his clown paint. He squeezed the mask, then held it against his cheek, like a comforting security blanket. Panting, he finally let it fall to the floor.

His broad shoulders rounded. His head felt heavy. His legs shook. What was he without the mask? With it, he was all powerful. He was a god who could strike fear into his victims. With it, he was an artist who could reshape humans into masterpieces.

He shook his head. *No, don't give in to those thoughts.*

Doctor Leyana reached up and stroked his curly brown hair. Her hands still shook. Her voice still cracked. "There's the Billy I know. He's not a monster. He's a good boy. Now, there's one more thing you have to do, Billy, so that we can begin your recovery."

He lowered his head to his chest. "What Doc?"

She placed a finger under his chin and gently lifted his head. "You have to turn yourself in to the police."

He shook his head violently. "Doc, no. Please don't make me do that. I'm afraid."

She extended a trembling finger. "You must be locked away if we are to contain the beast. Look at that young woman lying there in a pool of her own blood. You tore her to pieces, Billy, in a sick moment of vicious ecstasy."

Billy peered at the body.

He fell to his knees and crawled to the edge of the bloody puddle just an arm's reach from his victim. The heart he'd bitten into lay not far from the body. Her entrails hung from her insides and spread along the floor. Her eyes stared up vacantly to the ceiling.

Ripping off his blood-soaked gloves, he struck the side of his head over and over with his palms. What was he supposed to feel? *Damn me. I hate myself.* At the same time, blood flowed faster through his veins. He breathed deeper. The tingling returned. There was no denying he was an artist. "No, that's what the beast thinks. You have to—"

The dead woman gasped. Her head slowly turned to face him. Her eyes blinked. She smiled at him, a mix of blood and black goo sliding down her lips. *"Billy, thank you for this gift. I am so beautiful now. Come and give me a hug."* Her voice was deep and gargled. More ooze dropped from her lips. She held out her arms to him.

Billy stumbled backward. His eyes bulged. The blood rushed from his face. "No, this can't be."

"Billy what is it?" Doctor Leyana asked.

Billy pointed at the dead woman. She slowly climbed to her feet, her body cracking with each jerky movement. Her shredded skin hung loosely. Her bloody chest bones spread wider, revealing the empty cavity of her insides. "Look, she's standing up. Don't you see her? She's calling to me."

Doctor Leyana backed away. "Billy, no. It's your mind. It's twisting your vision. You have to co—"

The dead woman bent down and scooped up her own entrails with one hand. With the other, she lifted up her heart and held it out to Billy. *"Don't you want my heart, Billy? You wanted it before. You can have it. I belong to you now."* She staggered toward him. *"Come and give me a kiss."*

Heart racing, gasping for a breath, he crawled to Doctor Leyana and hid behind her legs. "Save me, please save me. She's coming for me."

Doctor Leyana shook her head. "You're wrong, Billy. Look at her, she's dead… just lying there how you left her."

The dead woman thrust her heart back into her chest. It slid down her exposed insides and dropped to the floor. She didn't notice. Her eyes were locked on him. She raised her hand to her mouth and licked the blood from her fingers, then caressed her cracked chest bones. *"Billy, don't be bashful. Give me a kiss."*

"No, stay away from me." Billy grabbed hold of Doctor Leyana's hand, then ran from the office, tugging her with him.

"Please, Billy, let me go," she pleaded, twisting her wrist back and forth and pounding on his hand with her fist.

"No, we have to hide." Dragging her through a darkened hallway, passing one locked door after another, he finally spotted a bathroom. "There, we can hide in there."

He shoved open the bathroom door and pulled her inside. His mouth dropped open. Doctor Leyana shrieked. He squeezed her wrist tighter. *What have I done?* The bathroom walls and mirrors were covered in blood. Shattered lights overhead flickered, providing only a dim yellow glow, but it was enough to see the mutilation the beast inside him unleashed.

A woman's body, her head nearly severed and hanging loosely from her neck, revealing the pulpy, torn insides of her throat, lay underneath one bathroom stall. Blood leaked from a gash in her stomach, spreading around her, soaking into her pantsuit. The bathroom stunk of urine and rotten eggs. Billy gagged. His gut convulsed. He bent over and couldn't stop the vomit.

"Billy, oh my God." Doctor Leyana thrashed her wrist to free herself, but he still wouldn't let go.

Gasping for air, wiping spew from his mouth with his free hand, he turned to her. "Doc, it's not me. I don't even remember doing this. It's the beast inside. I thought I could control it, like you taught me. Oh, what have I done? Help me, Doc. Please help—"

The woman underneath the stall began to moan. Her head twisted around unnaturally to face him. *"Billy, come and join me."* Slowly, she slid from the stall, then crawled toward him, her legs limply dragging behind her. Her head drooped against her chest, barely clinging to her shoulders. *"You hurt me, Billy. The pain is so exquisite. Now it's your turn to feel it."*

Billy released his grip on Doctor Leyana. She slivered to the corner, whimpering, covering her eyes with her hands.

"She's coming for me, Doc. You see her, don't you?" Billy retreated to the door, yanking on his hair with both hands.

Doctor Leyana shook her head. She mashed her body against the far wall. "No, Billy, all I see is you and that poor woman you butchered lying there dead."

"You're lying," he sobbed. "Why are you lying to me?"

"It's all in your head, Billy." Doctor Leyana inched toward him, her face grim, eyes blinking rapidly. "You have to end this insanity."

"I don't know how." Billy scrambled closer to the door.

The corpse crawling toward him was just an arm's length away. *"Billy, don't leave me. I'm your masterpiece, remember? You told me so as you cut through my neck over and over and watched me gasp my last breath."*

"No!" Billy turned and bolted from the bathroom, stumbling into the hallway, collapsing on all fours.

What had he done? What had he allowed the beast to do? How many had he killed? He couldn't remember. *You remember how it felt, though, don't you, Billy? You remember what it felt like to carve their bodies into art. Admit it, Billy.* He closed his eyes and shook his head. "No!" That was the beast talking, not him. Why had he let the beast out? *Don't give in to the fear, Billy. You can be the artist you were always meant to be. Just go and find your mask.* He opened his eyes. Yes, the beast was right. If he put the mask back on, he'd be safe. No one could harm him. He'd be the artist again.

Billy climbed to his feet and started toward the office where he'd dropped his mask and his dagger. He no longer sobbed. His insides felt warm again. He thrust out his chest, lifted his chin. His body vibrated with excitement. The dead couldn't hurt him. No one could. He was the artist. He was a go—"

Along the dimmed hallway, office doors slowly creaked open. The dead crossed through darkened entryways, unleashing guttural, pained moans. Billy's eyes bulged. A scream lodged in his throat. They were all women—four in all, each with their bodies twisted and mutilated by the beast. One's face was carved away with surgical precision. Another had the skin along her arms and legs sliced off, revealing muscles and tendons underneath. A third had her eyes and tongue torn out and her neck slashed. The fourth was the blond woman he'd flayed.

"Billy, don't leave us," they all chanted. *"Come and admire your artwork."*

"No, leave me alone." He slumped to his knees.

Beside him, the bathroom door opened just a crack. A bloody hand extended through the opening. *"Billy, stay with us forever,"* an anguished voice inside uttered. The door opened wider. The nearly severed head of the woman he'd killed there peaked out, her lips parted in a wide grin. *"Billy, don't you love your creations?"*

Billy buried his head in his chest and slammed his fists against his thighs. "Forgive me for what I've done? I couldn't control the beast."

"Join us, Billy." Each corpse lumbered toward him, hands outstretched.

From behind him, an elevator door pinged. He turned toward it, running clumsily down the hallway. Yes, if he could get down to the lobby, he could escape. He reached the elevator just as the doors slid open. Peering back, the dead women limped toward him, slowly closing the distance, moaning and chanting his name over and over.

The doors slid all the way open. Billy swung around to enter. A rather large man dressed in security guard clothing rushed through the door, tackling Billy. Together, they crashed to the floor, the security guard on top of him. Billy, thrashing his arms and legs, gazed into the man's face. He had no eyes. They'd been cut out, leaving vacant sockets. Blood seeped from the man's slashed neck, dripping over Billy's army green overcoat.

"Look what you did to me, Billy. The security guard blindly reached for Billy's face, his voice garbled as if his

lungs were filled with blood and liquid. *"You took my eyes, Billy. Why? You didn't have to do that. You could have killed me but left my eyes."*

"I'm sorry." Billy pushed the security guard off him. Scrambling to his feet, he spotted the door leading to the stairwell. Smashing his shoulder into the door, he burst through into a narrow passageway to the lobby. Flickering lights cast shadows over the walls. He breathed so fast his lungs were on fire. Each beat of his heart was like a sledgehammer smashing against his chest. His thoughts spun out of control. The beast told him to continue killing. His voice of reason told him to run away. His body shook. What was he, the merciless killer or the victim? He didn't know anymore.

Running down the winding stairs from the fourth floor down to the second, he suddenly stopped. Blood dripped from the walls onto the banister and the stairs. There was just a little at first, but then the flow increased until it spilled from the ceiling, like a flood, blocking his way to the lobby.

"No, this isn't real. It can't be real." He clutched his head and blinked his eyes, but the sea of blood remained.

Voices echoed around him. *"Billy, you cannot leave us."*

He covered his ears and threw open the stairwell door leading to the second floor. Maybe he could reach the elevator from there and escape to the lobby. The hallway was shrouded by a wall of blackness that limited his vision to just a few feet in front of him. His hands out in front of him, he staggered forward in search of the elevators.

"Billy, is that you?" a familiar voice uttered.

He froze. His heart danced. "Dr. Leyana, thank God. I hear you, but I can't see you. Save me, Doc. Take me away from this place. Save me from the others. I'll turn myself in to the police. I'll do anything you want me to. Just make me well again."

"Take my hand, Billy. There's only you and me here. No one else. You're safe." Doctor Leyana extended a hand through the darkness. "It'll be okay. Trust me."

Billy nodded. A sense of calm washed over him. "I've always trusted you, Doc. You were the only who understood me."

He grabbed her hand, and she tugged him through the murkiness until he could see her face. She smiled like she always did at him, her freckled cheeks a soothing reminder that one woman in his life cared about him.

"Thank you, Doc." He reached out to embrace her.

She drove his dagger through his heart, once, twice, three times, the blade tearing through his flesh over and over again until it no longer hurt. She screamed madly as she thrust the blade into him. Blood squirted from his chest onto her face, hair and her blouse. Billy slumped to the floor, wheezing out shallow breaths.

When she was finished, Doctor Leyana, covered in his blood, gasped for a breath. Her eyes bulged. Her chest heaved. She tilted her head and bent down to him. "Billy, this was the only way to cut out the beast inside of you."

He glared at her. She was right. She was so beautiful, but even as his life slipped away, he couldn't stop thinking how much more beautiful she would be if she were cut open, her insides exposed for all to see. Yes, she was right. The beast had to be put down. He coughed up blood. A chill spread through his body.

From somewhere close by, an elevator pinged, and the doors swished open.

"Now, you can join us, Billy. You can be art, just like us." The dead slithered toward him. He could hear their feet dragging along the hallway.

With his final breath, his vision dimming forever, he saw the dead fall upon him, their hands tearing into his chest.

***

"It's him all right, detective. It's Doctor William Bishop." Sergeant Torrance stood next to Detective Lowrey, both of them studying the mutilated body, chest ripped open with the heart torn out, discovered by the building's management company.

Detective Lowrey bent down to the body. "So, let me get this straight, sergeant. Somehow, our friend here, Doctor Bishop, who was the primary suspect in last year's massacre here at the Leyana Medical Building, broke in last night exactly a year later to the day, and now he's this mess of torn flesh we see before us."

Sergeant Torrance cleared his throat. "Yes, sir."

Detective Lowrey peered up at the sergeant. "And there's no security footage?"

"The building's been shuttered ever since the killings last year, and there's no power right now." Sergeant Torrance swallowed a bit of saliva.

Detective Lowrey scratched his beard and stood back up. "And there's no sign of struggle? There's no murder weapon? No other bodies in the building? It's just this torn-to-shreds body I see here before me."

"Yes, sir."

"Remind me sergeant about what exactly happened here a year ago?"

Sergeant Torrance raised an eyebrow. "Sir, Doctor Bishop, the deceased, who was a lead emergency room physician at Holy Cross Medical Center a few blocks away until a year ago, was a long-time patient of Doctor Beverly Leyana, a prominent psychiatrist and head of the Leyana Medical Group and owner of this building."

Detective Lowrey started jotting down notes in his pad. "Go on."

"We know from our investigation last year, that she was treating Doctor Bishop—she referred to him as Billy in her notes—for what she diagnosed as having a number of major psychosis disorders."

Detective Lowrey sighed. "Okay, get to the part where it gets bloody."

"On the night of September 18, one year ago yesterday, Doctor Bishop is suspected of having gone on a killing spree, targeting women. He killed five women at various locations around the city and then six women here at the Leyana Medical Building. He mutilated every single woman he killed. He also killed a security guard at the building."

"All of this in a day, sergeant?"

"Yes, sir."

"And how do we know it was Doctor Bishop who was responsible?" The detective peered over his pad at the sergeant.

"When we searched his office, we found writings describing what he planned to do in great detail. He wrote of wanting to turn the human body into art and to taste the blood of his artwork."

"Shit," Detective Lowrey blurted. "And you're telling me that somehow, after his freaking killing spree, he just escaped and was never seen or heard from again until last night when perhaps out or remorse or just plain craziness, he broke into an empty abandoned building, the very same building where he killed those women a year ago? Is that what you're telling me?"

"There's more, sir."

"I bet there is."

Sergeant Torrance motioned for the detective to follow him. He led the detective into an office on the second floor. "Sir, this was Doctor Leyana's office, and we found this brown bag on her desk.

Detective Lowrey peaked inside. What he saw made his eyes bulge. Inside was a mask made of what looked like human skin, painted to look like a clown... and the well-preserved head of a redhaired woman in a glass box."

"And who is this?" the detective asked?

"We're pretty sure it's Doctor Leyana," the sergeant answered. "That night a year ago, she was among those he killed, but we only found her headless body."

The detective shivered, and he never shivered from a case. "And you suspect Billy here had the head this whole time and brought it back to the building on the anniversary of her killing?"

"We did find his prints on the bag, sir."

"All right then, sergeant, so who killed our boy Billy last night? Who tore him to pieces? He couldn't have mutilated himself."

"No sir, he couldn't have." The sergeant glanced inside the bag. Doctor Leyana's eyes were open wide.

Had they been open before?

DABBLER

Shawn D. Brink

The Camaro fishtailed. Dustin overcorrected, lost control, and slammed into the culvert, back-end first.

He sat there, white knuckling the steering wheel as sweat trickled down his face. He pressed the accelerator, but the car wouldn't budge.

He cut the engine and tried opening the driver's door, but it was against the culvert's bank. So, he wriggled to the passenger side, opened the door and rolled out of the car, landing hard with his legs splayed out before him.

Despite sitting in about six inches of cold water, he didn't move. Instead, he cocked his head and listened.

The night was quiet except for the Camaro's engine, which ticked as it cooled. *Tick, tick, tick…*

Dustin scrambled from the ditch, staying low as he emerged onto the minimum-maintenance dirt road. Then, he froze and listened once more.

Tick, tick, tick…, went the Camaro. All else was silent.

There were no city lights out here in the boondocks and clouds hid the moon and stars. The only light came from the Camaro's headlights which shone into the woods across the road.

A gust rustled the leaves and drew a shiver from Dustin. His skin prickled with gooseflesh. He forced calming breaths.

The wind died, but Dustin's chill remained. The Camaro only ticked sporadically now. *Tick.........................tick.................................tick.*

A loud screech came from above and Dustin careened into the woods like a madman. He knew now that not even his Camaro was fast enough to shake that which hunted him.

The screeching grew louder as the creature drew nearer. Then, another noise, the beating of large wings – *thump, thump, thump...*

Here in the woods, everything was dark. The only light was the residual glow from the Camaro's headlights. But those beams splintered again and again as they shown through the trees, growing weaker and weaker as he fled deeper and deeper into the woods.

He flung himself through thick foliage. Twigs and thorns ripped his clothes and skin, but he dared not slow down.

Thump, thump, thump, those wings beat the air. Branches snapped and fell as the predator descended through the forest's canopy.

Dustin flew through the overgrowth, glancing back just in time to see it land. The Camaro's fractured light outlined its form – its hideous form.

Standing among the trees, it pulled its bat-like wings into itself and lifted its lupine nose to the sky. It stood upright to a height of at least eight feet. Its eyes glowed red like the fires of Hell. They were searching, probing eyes.

Dustin dove behind an outgrowth of ferns. He breathed through his mouth, controlling his lungs and forcing his body not to tremble.

It sniffed long and loud. A new sound came from it – something akin to a growling laugh. It began walking directly toward Dustin, slowly at first, but then faster.

Dustin bolted! Dead leaves crunched under his feet, but he hardly heard them over the screeching of his pursuer.

He sprinted through the woods. Something scratched the nape of his neck. He felt hot fingers begin to make their way around his collar, advancing over his jugular. Just then, the ground beneath him disappeared and the creature lost its hold.

Dustin fell down a steep embankment, landing in deep water. By the time he surfaced, the river's strong current had taken him a fair distance.

He could see its red eyes glaring at him. It tried to follow, but many low-hanging branches hindered its pursuit.

By some miracle, Dustin found an exposed tree root and held fast. He pulled himself out of the water and onto the far bank. Here, the tall river grass hid him.

He lay there, catching his breath. He could hear the creature crashing through the forest, growing nearer by the second. Dustin rose and fled deeper into the woods. He had to create distance. That was his only goal – his only hope.

Off to one side, he noticed light shining through the trees. He veered that direction and entered a clearing. There, a man sat on a log, reading a book next to a campfire.

"Who are you?" the man asked, looking up from his book.

Dustin had no breath for a reply.

"Why are you here?"

It all started with Raven.

***

Raven and Dustin attended the same high school, although they were not in the same grade. She was a year younger.

Dustin had a thing for Raven. Her jet-black hair was long and healthy, an asset that contrasted well with her fair skin. Also, she was a witch, a fact that intrigued him. His parents would never approve of her. Maybe though, that was part of the attraction.

Becoming involved with a witch was no big deal. Dustin wasn't a Bible-thumper, but he did belong to a church. Or, more precisely, he belonged to his parents' church. These days though, he rarely attended services or read his Bible.

"Have you ever participated in a séance?" she asked him one Friday afternoon between classes.

He shook his head.

"Well, I have. Did you know a little boy died under the old railroad bridge south of town?"

"When?"

"Long ago," she answered. "His spirit still roams the land."

Dustin's interest was piqued. "How do you know that?"

She laughed. "I've spoken with him before, out by the old bridge. He says if I come next time with a friend, then our combined aura will pull him across the veil more completely."

Dustin nodded, thinking it over. "And that's something we want?"

"Of course, silly," Raven batted her lashes. "Don't you want to get to know somebody like that? I mean, think of all the knowledge somebody like that would have about what's beyond this life." She paused. "Think of what he could teach us."

Dustin thought it over.

"So, do you want to do the séance with me?"

He nodded.

"Cool. Meet me under the bridge at dusk. See you then."

***

"We've got to get out of here now!" Dustin managed to shout between gasps. "Where's your car?"

The man didn't move from his log. He didn't say a word. He simply stared.

"You speak English?" Dustin shouted. "WHERE IS YOUR CAR!"

***

Dustin drove his Camaro along a dirt path that was little more than two tire ruts with weeds growing between them. These roads were rarely traveled these days. Back before the railroad left, they were used more. But that was long ago, years before Dustin was even born.

Ahead, the old railroad bridge rose into view. It looked black against the orange glow of the setting sun. Beneath it, a single figure – *Raven*.

She waved as he parked along the edge of the road, and his heartrate quickened. Silhouetted against the twilight, she looked absolutely beautiful.

Witchcraft is of the Devil! That's what Pastor preached once from the pulpit of his parents' church. Now though, those words were only a distant memory, almost nonexistent.

He approached. She was sitting cross-legged on the ground under the bridge.

"Hi," she said, looking up.

She gestured for him to sit in front of her, which he did. She was wearing black leggings and matching t-shirt. A gossamer-thin veil of black tulle hung over her head and down her body almost to the ground.

"I'm glad you came." Her voice was pleasant — relaxed.

His phone buzzed. He pulled it from his pocket. It was his mom. She was wishing him a fun night at the movies because that's where he told her he'd be.

"That's going to be a distraction," Raven said.

"What is?" he asked as he responded with a heart emoji to his mother.

"Turn your phone off and toss it over there by mine." She indicated a grassy spot a few feet away.

He did as she asked.

"Thank you."

Dustin smiled. "So, how does this work?"

"I'll do most of the heavy lifting," she said. "All you need to do is keep hold of my hands, relax, and stay within the circle."

The circle? It was drawn in the dirt around them. He scooted in to make sure he was well within its borders, and also as an excuse to scoot closer to her.

"The circle is power," she said. "Protective power."

"I thought we were just going to talk to a little boy?"

She nodded. "We are."

"Then, why the added protection?"

Raven laughed. "Oh brother, you don't dabble much in this sort of thing, do you?"

Dustin blushed.

"The circle is a precaution. We're only going to part the veil enough to speak with the child. But more lurks there than children. If anything else tries to push through, I'll shut the portal. But, if by slim chance something escapes, this circle will protect us."

Dustin nodded. *Witchcraft is of the Devil!* Pastor's voice echoed so weakly in his mind that it went unheeded.

***

"We've got to get out of here!"

The man didn't move, not one muscle. He just sat there with the book open in his hands, staring.

"Now!"

"I know who you are," the man said. "You have the stench of a dabbler."

"Look, something is coming! It will kill both of us if it catches us! We've got to go now!"

"Listen up, dabbler. Hear the words of the Lord," the man said, looking down at his book. "I know your deeds, that you are neither cold nor hot. I wish you were either one or the other! So, because you are lukewarm – neither hot nor cold – I am about to spit you out of my mouth.”

“We don't have time for this!” Dustin screamed.

“There's always time for God.” The man remained seated. “You must choose. God doesn't do lukewarm. You must be hot or cold.”

Somewhere beyond the clearing, the creature screeched. Time was running out!

It screeched again – louder, closer.

***

Raven smiled. “Close your eyes, sweetie.”

He liked her calling him that. He closed his eyes.

“No peeking.”

He felt her hands take hold of his. They were warm in his grip, inviting.

“Little boy from beyond the veil,” she said with barely more than a whisper. “Are you there?”

Dustin listened hard but heard nothing.

“Little boy?” Raven said a bit louder. “Are you there?”

Just silence.

He felt her fingers twitch in his hands. "I'm getting something. Do you feel it?" she asked.

Besides her twitching fingers, Dustin felt nothing. He snuck a peek.

She remained seated with her eyes shut tight. Her lips quivered slightly. The black-tulle veil fluttered minutely as she breathed in and out.

"I'm getting a name," she said.

"Who's?" Dustin wanted to know.

"Him."

"The boy?"

Raven didn't respond.

"Are you getting the boy's name?" The suspense was killing him.

Her voice grew fearful. "No."

Her hands began to tremble, growing cold and clammy. Her eyes remained tightly shut – so tight that her brow furrowed.

"It's not the boy!" she blurted. "It's...It's...Nooooo!"

"Who is it?" Dustin said, his voice rising.

"I – I can't shut the portal. It won't let me!" Raven sobbed.

He pried his hands loose and grabbed her by the shoulders, shaking her gently.

She didn't open her eyes. Her brow furrowed deeper.

Dustin shook her harder. "This isn't funny, Raven! Wake up!"

"It's…he's…"

An otherworldly screech boomed.

Dustin let go of her and jumped to his feet. The screech came again, and he spun toward it.

Not more than ten feet away, among the deepest shadows under the bridge, a new shadow emerged.

Raven shrieked! He turned back to her. Her eyes were wide open now. She screamed, clawing her face, snagging her nails on the veil and drawing streaks of blood from her flushed cheeks.

"It's not the boy!" she wailed.

She pointed, and Dustin's eyes followed that trembling finger's trajectory. He watched in terror as the new shadow gained form and solidity. It stood there, red eyes aglow, unfurling bat-like wings and staring directly at him.

"Stay in the circle!" Raven shouted.

But Dustin, in his panic, had already fled. He was almost certain that circles in the dirt couldn't save him anyway – *not from that!*

He ran toward his car!

And the creature gave chase.

***

Saplings snapped. Branches broke. The creature entered the clearing.

Dustin screamed!

The camper remained seated on his log. "Are you going to be hot, cold, or just lukewarm? You must decide NOW!"

The man's voice sounded distant as Dustin's sanity teetered.

"You cannot drink the cup of the Lord and the cup of demons too!" he shouted at Dustin.

The demon stepped forward, walking right through the fire. Embers sparked where he stepped. Flames stoked around him.

"You cannot have a place at both the Lord's table and the table of demons."[2]

"Help me!" Dustin shouted.

The man answered from where he sat, "I'm only a servant. I can't help you unless you ask my master."

"Shut up!" the demon's voice was guttural.

"Ask my master for help!" the man said.

"I said shut up!" the demon spat.

"Who is your master?" Dustin desperately wanted to know.

The man's voice was like thunder. "Here I sit, holding God's word in my hands, quoting scripture – and you dare ask, who is my master?"

The demon glared at Dustin. "I'm your master. You and the witch called me forth. Now, you belong to me!"

"Don't listen to his lies!" the man boomed. "Ask and you shall receive!"

Dustin shook. Fear planted him.

"You receive not, because you ask not!" the man bellowed.

The demon shouted. "You are mine forever!"

Dustin dropped to his knees. One name entered his mind. It was the name his parents' paster always called on.

"Save me Jesus!!!" Dustin screamed just as the demon lunged with its gnarled claws extended.

But those claws never sank into Dustin's flesh. They were stopped by the man on the log. Only, he was no longer on the log. And he wasn't a man.

His appearance changed as he moved between the demon and Dustin. A bright-white light shone from him. It washed out the demon, making him pale by comparison.

Wings unfurled from the angel's back, spreading like those of a giant eagle. He shoved the demon away and simultaneously drew an enormous flaming sword.

"You have no right to take my prize!" the demon spat as it prowled the edge of the clearing.

The angel's voice shook the ground. "All who call on the name of the Lord shall be saved. He will not be judged but has crossed over from death to life."[6]

The demon shrieked, staring at the angel with dread-filled eyes. Then, it turned and fled into the woods. The angel gave chase.

Alone, Dustin stared at the dying campfire. The angel's Bible sat on the now-vacant log. He picked it up, sat on the log, bowed his head, closed his eyes, and spoke with God for the first time in a long time. It was a conversation full of sincerity and tears.

Finally, he opened his eyes and looked toward the eastern horizon. The sun was rising.

It was Saturday morning and Dustin began walking back toward the car. If he couldn't get it out of the ditch, he'd walk to town.

And once in town, he'd walk directly to church. He was eager to recommit his life to the Lord. He yearned to learn more of what it means to be saved by Jesus.

Also, he needed to find out when Sunday service started because he didn't want to be late, ever.

HIGHWAY TO HELL

Ric Wasley

The night that Stefano (Stiggy) Rizzo died was unremarkable.

The night he returned from the dead wasn't.

Oddly enough (or maybe not) both events took place at the same location. A seedy hole-in-the-wall dive called "Sal's" in Brooklyn's Flatbush neighborhood that served as a home-away-from-home for both petty criminals and cockroaches in just about equal numbers in both conviviality and personal hygiene.

"Sal's" and Stiggy Rizzo were a perfect fit. In fact, if "Sal's" current owner - a 320 lb mountain of jelly and indifference ironically known as Minuscolo or Mini for short, had been looking for a poster boy that most typified the ambiance and clientele he could have done no better than to hang Stiggy's portrait in a place of honor over the bar.

Ironically that is exactly what had happened the night that Stiggy returned from the dead - which on account of Stiggy having snuffed it right there the night before was the least Mini felt he could do.

***

It was also, coincidentally, the night that Stiggy graduated from petty theft, car-jacking, and aggravated assault to a double homicide in the form of an aggrieved former dope dealing partner who felt he'd been cheated by Stiggy claiming the heroin he sold him had been over-cut with Quinine - which was unfair. While there was some Quinine used in the cut it was mostly cornstarch, which tended to coagulate in the cheap needles their junkie clientele used and make for very unsatisfied customers.

Thus, as shit tends to flow downward Stiggy's much-abused exfriend and partner came literally gunning for him and in a brief exchange of four-letter words centered around illegitimate antecedents and descendants ended with Stefano "Stiggy" Rizzo's brains being distributed all over the PBR and Bud taps at the center of the bar.

The next night, with the felon arrested and the bar taps wiped down with Clorox and Pine Sol, it turned into just another typical night at Sal's... which is to say both boring and depressing in equal measure.

One of the late and mostly unlamented of Stiggy's friends had suggested that said depressing collection of drunks and junkies at the bar raise a toast to the sneering face of the recently deceased's photo hanging askew over the bar.

Rather than a salute of glasses and long top bottles the suggestion had been met by a derisive chorus of rude noises punctuated by the occasional, "fuck you."

Stiggy in death was even less popular than he'd been in life.

However, the mere act of voicing an "F-U" or releasing a belch in spiritual support of the sentiment left a temporary void of silence that was unexpectedly filled by a redolent, "Well then fuck you too." Which caused the heads not already passed out on the bar to blearily turn to the source of the sound.

Although those who saw who'd uttered that simple but effective sentence would forever after regard it as their most probably undeserved 15 minutes of fame, few if any, registered just what they were seeing.

The late Stiggy Rizzo's best... and that would be stretching it... "friend", Devo, probably summed it up best. "Whaaaat?"

Because leaning against the peeling paint wall that maybe once had been white was the spitting image of the late and curiously unlamented man in question, Stefano "Stiggy" Rizzo.

Had there been more patrons that night who had not been more than nine-tenths stoned there might have been panic at seeing the ghost of the petty thug who'd bought the farm only 24 hours previously. But most just shook their heads before putting them back down at the bar, grateful that it wasn't the small slimy rodents or insects that usually accompanied their delirium trauma dreams.

Thus, it was left to one of the few semi-comatose spectators, Mini himself, to state the obvious.

"What the fuck...? You're supposed to be dead!"

To which the late and largely unlamented Stiggy, shrugged his bony shoulders and responded, "Yeah, no shit!"

***

That, as the rest of the world knows all too well, was where the legend of Stiggy Rizzo began. But as scientists, philosophers, statesmen and numerous ecclesiastical scholars of multi-denominational persuasions have speculated... it was most certainly not where it ended.

Far from it.

In fact, it was just the beginning of a phenomenon that would sweep the entire sphere of human existence in alarmingly short order.

But people being people there is nothing humanity craves more than a good story... unless it's one that is accompanied by an enticing helping of bullshit wrapped up in a beguiling red ribbon of plausible promise.

Because that was what the miracle of Stiggy, 'The Boy from Beyond', became.

Let's face it, every religion since the first caveman got his brains bashed out by a wooly mammoth has promised its grieving adherents that death is not the final nail in the spiritual coffin.

But outside of a few - think Christianity... and that one only one, though significant, appearance of resurrection, most have failed to deliver concrete, measurable, and empirical... proof.

But Stiggy Rizzo changed all that.

***

After getting over his initial shock the still bemused 'Mini' watched in skeptical silence as the aforementioned Stiggy hoisted his skinny butt onto his regular barstool and ordered Bud long-neck.

"Five bucks," said 'Mini' automatically...loath to extend the long overdue bar tab by one red cent - resurrection miracle or not.

But Stiggy wasn't letting his newfound status go to waste.

"What the fuck Mini, this is the way you greet the guy who's just come back from the dead? What a dick!"

When put that way, what else could the corpulent bartender do but shrug and add the watery Bud to the apparently eternal tab and push a dirty glass in the revenant's direction.

And it all might have ended there if not for a stroke of providence, dumb luck, or divine serendipity, depending on your degree of credibility.

Because sitting in a dingy corner of the even dingier nondescript bar was a nascent future alcoholic about-to-be washout from the Fourth Estate, Damon Murray. Damon had once been a rising star of the journalistic world when he scored a coveted internship on the NYT city desk upon graduation from Columbia.

And for a while, it looked like his star was on the assent as he fetched and carried in the hunt for salacious details about racist congressmen, homophobic city councilors, and anti-LBGTQ school board protesters. He'd even gotten a commendation from the 'TsGCATH' (Trans-Global Collation Against Transphobic Homophobes). As Tom Pretty sang... "The sky was the limit.."

Until... that fateful night.

In a horrible twist of malevolent fate, it was at the very same event that that the dewy-eyed and fatally innocent Damon was to receive his 'TsGCATH' award in the form of a golden, and as some would unkindly remark, vaguely phallic gilt painted lump of rainbow striped plastic.

As the NYT's newly promoted city desk reporter collected the cheesy recognition of laudable adherence to the prevailing political correctness, he couldn't help but notice the beaming smile of his immediate superior, Chesley Van Husten, and his beguiling, and twenty-five years junior, wife. The ex-semi-super model Alicia Sims-Silverstein, of whom, if the NYT salacious grape-vine could be believed was also an insatiable predator of anything of any gender that could remind her of her rapidly fading adorable ingenue status.

Alicia SS, as the tabloids had dubbed her, had burst on the jaded scene of over-sexed teen seductresses by bedding her first conquest, an aging jail-bait Tween model photographer and agent at the age of 12. Her mother had reportedly been pitching a reprise of the famous Brook Shields "Pretty Baby" layout in the hope that a modern Calvin Kline would have their salacious socks blown off by the sultry middle school siren.

After a few frank conversations revolving around jail bait and jail time, the well-connected paparazzi, who shortly retired to Vermont to raise Zucchini and erotically suggestive butternut squashes, did come through with an introduction and subsequent contract to Teen Vogue.

For the next ten years not only was Alicia SS a pop phenomenon, it was all but impossible to go anywhere in the civilized world (and much of the not-so-civilized) without seeing her baby blues and perky buttocks gracing a cover of some magazine, tabloid or billboard.

She hung with every drugged-out, narcissistic brat/rat pack that Hollywood could dredge up. She toured with Taylor and ran through NFL and NBA studs like they were meth bonbons at a Malibu weekend bash.

It was only when she reached the ripe old age of twenty-three and her mother snarkily pointed to a minuscule patch of cellulite marring the here-to-fore flawless butt of the former teen lust inducer that she began to think of the future in terms other than whom could she bed and where for how much.

That's why when she met the aging Lothario and remarkably vapid egotist, one Chesley Van Huston, she decided that rather than fuck him and forget him, as was her usual modus operandi, the vain but attractively endowed trust-fund patrician might prove to be a good hedge against the inevitable looming of the conqueror worm in the form of future cellulite and sagging boobs.

Armed with those romantic thoughts she'd pursued and wed the pompous would-be progenitor of a new generation of overprivileged and under-talented denizens of the Upper East Side and the Hamptons.

It hadn't really worked out. For a number of reasons, which the hapless and prematurely happy Damon Murray found out that fateful night.

As he walked back to the head table clutching his disturbingly phallic major award, his boss, Chesley Van H, put an arm around him and drawled in his New England prep school faux British accent, "Well done my boy. The Grey Lady is proud of you."

Damon beamed back but his smile was not for the grey-templed face next to his, it was for the sultry do-me smile playing across the pouty glistening lips of the pretentious patrician's bride.

Thus when Mr. Van H Esq. suggested they repair to their toney Upper East Side townhouse Damon's head filled with fantasies of intimate invitations and unbridled lust.

He was half right.

***

Damon stared gloomily at the depressing motif of the equally depressing bar and wondered for the hundredth time how he could have been so stupid.

Yes, he'd been a rather naive kid from the Midwest when he'd shown up at Columbia his freshman year but four years of undergrad and another of Masters should have provided ample time and acumen to the twisted morals of NYC.

Why then had he stumbled so blindly into the sleazily decadent swamp that was the prurient playground of the Upper East Side elites to whom the pursuit of perversion was second only to their trust funds?

At first, he was convinced that his original assessment of the lusty looks he'd been getting from the former teen tease hottie had been correct.

All the way back to their exclusive digs she'd nuzzled up next to him in the limo and by the time they'd pulled up to the building and the doorman opened the limo door, he'd been frantically trying to get his seat belt unbuckled and pants buckled up again.

Half dazed with a cut crystal glass of limo-bar single malt scotch he'd snuggled next to her in the small elevator and into the luxurious penthouse apartment grinning from ear to ear.

Canapés and champagne had graced the bar and when Alicia SS reappeared from the bedroom clad in a black leather bustier accessorized by silver chains, 5-inch spiked heels, and a jeweled handled riding crop, all he could say was, "holy shit," and try not to let the drool from his dripping tongue stain his rented tuxedo.

"Hot damn!" he thought, "this will be a night to remember." And it was. Just not in the way he thought.

***

Damon took another pull of his 7&7 that he suspected contained neither real Seagrams or even 7-Up.

In fact, the only thing authentic about the drink was the fact than as near as he could tell the watery 7&7 mix in his hand was his 7th drink in the dump.

He laughed out loud and clacked the glass back down on the cheap Formica table.

The unusual occurrence of a sound coming from anywhere but the bar caused several patrons to turn their heads in his direction. And when he looked back he was rewarded with a, "What fuck you lookin' at?"

Being neither sober enough nor physically inclined toward violence Damon shrugged and returned to studying the dozens of rings the dirty glass had left on the even dirtier tabletop.

And that might have been the end of it except for the now heated conversation taking place at the bar where another of Stiggy's former dealers in crime was joining in the increasing skepticism of the formerly dead and now quick Stiggy's miraculous resurrection. Which was as Tommi-Boy, Tomas Sanchez, declared, "Bullshit".

There were nods all around and while a few of the mildly religious pointed out that Jesus did it, the consensus was that Stiggy was most certainly not him.

It was about this time that fate, in the form of the ever-present, "Put your money where your mouth is" guy, stepped into the bar.

"Yeah…" added Dom, Dominic Mazzacano. "This is some kind of a bullshit scam. It's one of those smoke and mirror tricks like the movie where the guys heist millions and it's all computer fakes and rubber masks."

Stiggy sighed theatrically, stung by his former stalwarts' lack of faith in his obvious miracle. "So whadd'a I got to do to convince you dumb fucks?"

"Prove it!" came the universal reply.

The die was cast.

***

It still could have ended right there had Stiggy just walked away and into the sweet bye-and-bye or oblivion… but then the world might never have changed and we might not all be… Oh well, let's continue.

***

Stiggy turned to Dom.

"OK numb-nuts, just how would you like me, to "prove it"?

"Do it again."

"Do what?"

"Kill yourself - blow your brains out. You know like the first time. If you're like fuckin' immortal, then do it again. Show us. Come on back from the dead."

Stiggy raised his eyebrows and drained his beer.

"Again?"

"Yeah... Again."

"And what's in it for me?"

"Well, shit. We'll believe you?"

Stiggy snorted. "Yeah, and that gets me off - how?"

"OK," said Dom. "Pool. Everyone pony up $20 for Mr. Miracle here to make it worth his while."

Stiggy looked around the twenty-odd patrons at the bar.

"Now I call bullshit. Four bills for blowing my own brains out...? Hell, I wouldn't piss on your shoes for that."

There was a brief muttered conference halfway down the bar.

"OK. Then we raise it. A 'C' note each. How's that work for you?"

Stiggy considered for a moment.

"I'm not sure money actually does much for you up there but hey, it at least shows you're serious, so yeah - OK." He turned and looked down the bar. "Who's got a piece?"

The was a lot of muttering but no one answered.

"OK," said Stiggy, "how 'bout a 'throw-down'?" A battered old snub nose .38 came skittering down the bar.

Stiggy picked it up.

"OK. So which one of you assholes wants to do it?"

"Do what?" Came the chorus.

Stiggy spun his empty long-neck bottle on the bar top and said, "Shoot me."

A damp miasma of silence spread over the bar.

Though no strangers to violence, even murder, done in dark alleys with shots on the back, from the assembled low lives, there were none... At least none who wanted to do it in front of twenty witnesses who would be only too happy to turn rat at some future date to cut a deal to lessen their own future culpability.

Stiggy got it.

He twirled the stubby revolver with the filed-off serial number around on the bar top until it stopped.

Everyone looked where it was pointed.

At a shadow of misery and hopelessness nursing a watery cheap whisky and no-name mixer at a grungy Formica table in the corner.

Bingo.

"Hey, you!"

The pathetic heap of despair didn't look up.

One of the Brooklyn barflies oozed off his stool and staggered over.

"Hey pal, check it out man, somebody's talkin' to you."

Damon only looked up because he had to take another drink and it was hard to swallow staring at the table.

"You wanna earn some fast cash?" Stiggy called from the bar.

Damon didn't care but was persuaded to answer by a beery whisper in his ear.

"Better say yes if you wanna' walk out of here without my foot up your ass."

He gave the only answer he could... "I don't give a shit."

"Good enough." smiled Stiggy, motioning to the bar, "Step this way to fame and fortune."

A painful twist of his ear by the Brooklyn booster motivated him up from the table and he made his unsteady way towards the knot of lowlifes clustering around a grinning Stiggy who held out a hand.

"Pleased to meetcha', I'm Stiggy, and you can help us settle a friendly bar bet."

Damon peered myopically at the pasty face that filled his vision and muttered fatalistically, "Whadda' I have to do?"

The words that would make him both famous and infamous came back with a grin, "Kill me."

***

Stiggy quickly filled the befuddled Damon in on the events of the past twenty-four hours and explained that the events in question could only be settled by Stiggy once more taking a bullet to the brain in front of enough credulous witnesses who could later verify and attest to his miraculous resurrection.

For performing this service the Brooklyn Barfly Association would pay him the princely sum of $437.33

which represented the sum total of the tangible assets the group could come up with at such short notice.

Still, despite the enticement of that princely sum, Damon might have chosen to resist their blandishments had it not been for the recent and all too painful events only hours before at the Upper East Side penthouse paradise of his former employer.

***

"Where's Chesley?" Damon asked nervously. Not because he wanted to see him but more because he was afraid his boss would walk in on them while the former Teen Vogue model was exploring his right ear canal with her tongue.

"Who cares?" she whispered seductively and began unbuttoning his shirt.

"Well, it's just that I wouldn't want him to walk in suddenly and think that we were going to ..."

"Fuck?" She laughed tossing his shirt to the floor. "Oh, but we are. Most definitely. Unless... you're not interested?"

She took a half step back and pouted in the same way that she had learned in puberty drove middle-aged men wild.

Damon was no exception.

"Oh no - not at all. I mean I am. It's just that I wouldn't want him to walk in and get... upset."

She gave a husky laugh. "Trust me. He won't. In fact, he'd only get upset if we weren't." She smiled an impish grin. "Believe me, he has shall we say... 'Great Expectations', for you." She laughed and tugged at his belt buckle.

"Holy shit!" Damon thought. *"It's really happening. I'm about to get my first threesome!"* as erotic images of sweaty lust shimmered across his libido.

He was right... sort of.

Just as his pants joined his tie and shirt on the expensive Persian carpet the bedroom door opened behind him and a strangely soft but deceptively masculine voice lisped, "Oh goody, you've already started. I can't wait!"

A somewhat bemused Damon turned around and did a mildly comic double-take at the bizarre and wholly unexpected image draped in a sultry pose against the bedroom door.

A slinky sequined black cocktail dress set off by a diamond choker, black stockings, and 6-inch stiletto heels. Ruby red lips and deep purple eyeshadow crowned with long curling ringlets of platinum blond hair.

"Whaaaat? was all Damon could croak out.

"Oh Cherrie," tittered the surprisingly attractive crossdresser. "You don't even recognize me? That is just so, so sweet! I just knew when I picked you out that you were going to be so right for our... 'lifestyle'."

By this time Alicia was in the process of removing his boxer shorts so when his erstwhile boss and part-time crossdresser sauntered over and planted a big wet, sloppy French kiss on his slack-jawed mouth his entangled ankles wouldn't allow his to escape the embrace. So he did the only thing his former Eagle Scout small-town incarnation could think of. He hit him.

***

So now here he was, unemployed, and quite literally and figuratively crying into his beer - well 7&7 - and wondering how the hell he was going to pay his share of the rent on the 2 bedroom, not too clean, third-floor walk-up three blocks over that was due next week... just when his paycheck would not be forthcoming.

Thus, rather than politely declining the ridiculous offer and hauling ass out of there as he would have done just 24 hours (and a whole lot more sober) earlier, Damon picked up the battered revolver and eyed it.

"Well...?" Barfly #1 drawled out sarcastically. "Are you gonna do it or sit there with your dick in your hand all night?"

Maybe it was the sarcasm, or the booze, or his need for rent money - but most likely it was the comment concerning the part of his anatomy that had most cruelly betrayed him with the events on the Upper East Side but suddenly Damon snapped and snarled..."Fuck it!"

And pulled the trigger.

No one was more surprised than he when Stiggy's nose disappeared in a welter of blood, bone, and cartilage to the exclamations of, "Holy shit!" And, "What the fuck!" And, "Hey dude you got blood all over my jacket - you're paying the cleaning bill for that!"

But most simply stood over Stiggy's latest corpse with its bloody oatmeal face pooling gore onto the dirty linoleum tiles.

"Well, shit." commented Barfly #2, "I guess he's not coming back from this one." He pulled out a $50. "Any takers?"

There were none.

Five minutes later the cops showed up.

Still drunk and barely aware of what was happening, Damon was arrested, booked on 'Murder-One', and was standing in court the following morning about to be remitted to Rikers Island on 10 million cash bail when a grimy figure with bad teeth, greasy hair, and a slight odor of decay pushed his way toward the bench, calling out, "Hey man, let this dude go. No harm - no foul."

It was Stiggy.

***

This time the internet exploded. The conspiracy crew and paranormal pals were all over it.

And of course, local, citywide, and quickly national print and cable news were too.

There were at first a lot of, "No comments." from police, the DA, and a very embarrassed coroner's office when they slid open mortuary slab #37 to find the sheets rumpled and the corpse missing. Oops.

Not that it hadn't happened before but all of those had been the result of sloppy toe tags, mislaid files, or occasional necrophilia.

This time was different.

The stiff actually showed up in the court that was trying his murder case.

Except he wasn't a stiff and he wasn't murdered.

He was walking, talking, and back from the dead. No worse for wear other than some seriously bloodstained clothes and in dire need of some personal hygiene.

Oh, he was printed and scrutinized, and blood and DNA tested. He was poked, prodded, and peered at until he said, "Fuck this, I'm outta here," and left only to run into a street filled with paparazzi and microphones thrust into his face who wanted to know all about his miraculous brush with death.

Had he just been wounded?

No.

Could they see the wounds?

There were none.

Was he an imposter? Were the police hiding the real corpse of Stiggy Was the whole thing a hoax?

No.

No.

And…

No.

"Hey if you don't believe me, go ask the cops. Or better still go on down to Sal's and ask the crew. They saw it with their own eyes."

And they did. All of whom swore on a stack of bibles (like they'd ever picked one up) that they personally witnessed Stiggy getting his brains blown out just the night before.

"In fact," said the guy with the brain-spattered jacket, "I'm sending that dumb fuck the cleaning bill."

The on-the-spot news crews radioed back to the anchor at the courthouse. "Hey, quick, do an interview with... "That dumb fuck."

And so the hapless, hopeless, and semi-suicidal Damon found himself launched on the road to fame.

***

All of the major news networks and wire feeds rushed to not only swarm the resurrected Stiggy but that "dumb fuck who launched him to fame - the formerly unemployed, and recently black-balled, Damon.

Strangely enough - or maybe not so much, his former employer and scorned Transvestite lover, the recently miffed but now positively avuncular, City Desk

Editor, called him shortly after the headline breaking stories scorched their way around the world. Which was coincidently right after the NYT Editor-in-Chief head honcho made in a snarky call to City Desk inquiring why the Grey Lady had no-one Johnny-on-the-spot to compete with the rest of the ravenous 4th Estate.

Chesley mumbled something about getting right on it and all was well for about 15 minutes. Until an AP wire story came in mentioning the young man who launched the "Dude who came back from the Dead," which was what the press had christened Stiggy, as one Damon Murray, a *former* employee of the NYT City Desk.

That was when the upscale shit hit the elite fan and the soon-to-also-be 'former' City Desk Editor (unless he retrieved Damon) was on the phone to the still somewhat bemused recently at large reporter, making as nice as nice can be.

"So what do you say young Damon? Let's forget the recent unpleasantness and have you report back tomorrow AM at say a 50% salary increase?"

Though it was not a video call, Damon could see the supercilious grin oozing through the ether.

"What do I say? How does "fuck you", sound?"

You see Damon had a new job. He was now Stiggy's press liaison and manager.

***

Less than six hours into the new job he knew he was gonna need help.

The requests for interviews, both cable and print came faster than flies to uncollected garbage on a summer's day in Manhattan.

But after the first two… CNN and FOX, it became clear that once the first wave of 'phenomenon-of-the-moment' had settled, there was a nasty wave of skepticism beginning to arise.

This was mainly due to the less than credible reliability of the denizens of Sal's who had the collective believability of a bartender turned politician.

So it came as no surprise to Damon when an on-air "gotcha'" news anchor for NBC ambushed him and his new client with, "You are aware of course that many in the paranormal skeptic community are claiming that this is just another in the long series of hoaxes perpetrated on a gullible public to sell books and provide content fodder for all the UFO and ghost hunter fringe elements."

"Well," said Damon reasonably, "If you don't believe me, or the entire bar, who witnessed it… how do you propose we prove it?"

The perfectly coiffed and heavily made-up TV journalist smiled sweetly. "Do it again. Live, and on air."

***

The hunt for the proper venue took more than a week but after rejecting offers from Jimmy Kimmel, Stephen Colbert and The View it was decided that due to the major networks annoying requests for armies of lawyers, outrageous bonds and reams of paperwork, a local Cable station out of Brooklyn finally said that they would provide the backdrop and any other stations that cared to could pick up the live feed or simulcast it.

This was mainly due to Stiggy's insistence that the event be held at Sal's, the home to his previous pair of miraculous murders and subsequent resurrections.

On the appointed night the place was jammed with cable reporters, a few print stringers, a host of paranormal researchers and new-age bloggers. There were of course the locals but most were left outside and the few who had managed to get pulled in by Stiggy were still pissed that numerous other cousins, girlfriends, mom's and aunts had been unable to bull their way in as well.

By the time the 8 pm showtime rolled around Mini had long since run out of cheap draft and even the odd cases of cans and bottles that had conveniently 'fallen' off the delivery truck had run dry.

"OK, you ready?" A geeky looking producer with an i-pad pointed to a semicircle of folding chairs on a small, raised platform at the end of the bar.

Damon raised his eyebrows at Stiggy who grinned back and they took their seats as the producer clipped lapel mics to their shirts.

The local cable news gal, one Cherie Capezzi, smiled distractedly and said, "OK… so I'm gonna introduce you two, ask some background questions and then you'll take some questions from the…" She looked at her notes, "members of the paranormal community. And then…" she looked up and smiled nervously, "on to the main event."

Stiggy winked. "Right, when this dude blows my brains out."

She leaned forward and whispered nervously to Damon. "Is this going to be messy?"

Thinking back to the last time, he wormed his mind through the alcoholic haze of the previous event.

"Yeah, pretty much."

That led to a hurried discussion about plastic tarps which was ended when the producer shrugged and said, "Hey this isn't our studio, so no problem." And then added, "though If I were you, I'd stand back because brains do splatter."

Finally, it was time.

They had answered the questions, belabored the obvious, and now once again it was show time.

Damon answered questions, referred to his journalist background and gave enough oblique references to his less than amicable parting from the 'Grey Lady' to stick one satisfying jab up his former boss's patrician ass while Stiggy told of his life in Brooklyn in one or two nasal sentences that simply added up to, "not much".

Then it was the turn of the paranormal folks who with varying degrees of skepticism and irrational hope asked Stiggy about past lives, space aliens, spirits, ghosts, Bigfoot, and Atlantis.

Then it was time for the main event.

As a local cop hired for the event brought out a brand-new GLOCK 22 firing a .40 S&W cartridge, Damon realized he'd forgotten to ask if they'd like to have them standing or seated.

"Well, why don't you do it just like you did the last time so the audience can see exactly what everyone here witnessed."

"Sounds good to me," Stiggy said and elbowed his way up to the bar and slouched onto a stool.

He picked up a half-empty beer from the bar, drained it, belched, and winked, "Let's get it on."

***

The shot that blew Stiggy's brains out for the 3d time in less than two weeks, while expected, still made everyone jump and/or scream.

Damon held the smoking GLOCK, blinked a few times, bit his lower lip, and then handed the weapon back to the waiting cop.

The precinct homicide forensic squad moved in and efficiently slid Stiggy's still-seated corpse into a body bag, then onto a gurney and into a waiting ambulance to be transported to the morgue for autopsy and the pre-arranged vigil, that would determine if Stiggy remained a corpse or was truly able to come back from the other side as claimed.

Damon found out the next morning that considering the unexpected ratings and trending social media of the Stiggy execution previously uptight major networks had relaxed their strictures and sent some local teams to interview the forensic boys at the morgue.

But when the reports came back that Stiggy remained dead as the proverbial doornail they made a few bad jokes and went off to resign their copy to the 'man-bites-dog' file.

That's why none of them were there the following night at Sal's when Stiggy walked in at a bit after 8 pm and said, "Hey - where the fuck is everyone?"

The locals and the faithful forever after retained full smug bragging rights about being there when their local hometown hero proved conclusively that yes, Virginia, there is life after death.

***

The internet blew up - again.

Social media went wild.

Cable News went spastic and then slavering in their desperation to get Stiggy interviews and exclusives.

And suddenly Damon found himself fielding million-dollar offers.

At first, he was flattered, then overwhelmed and then he decided he needed help, lots of it.

So he quickly hired an assistant in the form of a copy editor he'd worked with who he'd been friendly in a platonic sort of way - which seemed the safest way to proceed if he was going to handle this as a business. Which he did by next hiring a hungry corporation lawyer who'd been one of his roommate's freshman year. He was bright and reasonably honest, for a lawyer, and promised not to pad his hours too outrageously.

He then rented an almost roach-free office over a Deli off of Flatbush Ave and posted a small fiberboard plaque that read 'Damon Murray - Public Relations'.

It was off to the races.

And the races began before the office lease was out of the printer. Kendra, his PA, told him two hours after their first phone line went live that she was missing five calls for everyone she could answer, and the voice mail was completely filled.

Same with their email account. And she couldn't even think about when she was going to have time to design a website.

So, Damon called back the three most aggressive cable news networks and told them Stiggy would give them interviews for double what they were offering - and all of upfront. They agreed all too quickly, and Damon learned the valuable lesson about leaving cash on the table and called his lawyer, Jason, telling him to handle all of the competing offers and financials and to pad his hours as much as he liked.

At the end of the first week, he'd made more money than he ever thought possible in a dozen lifetimes. Because everyone wanted Stiggy.

Oh, there were still skeptics but when the coroner who pronounced him dead and the pathologist who'd autopsied him testified at a hastily convened inquest concurred that the once dead Stiggy was now alive, most of the world pretty much got on board

And where was Stiggy in all this?

Still hanging out at Sal's.

Or trying to.

Naturally, those media outlets who didn't have the budgets to score one of those very pricey interview slots through Damon & Co. quickly tried to catch the media star of the millennium at his hangout, *in situ* as it were. But mostly, for, *gratis.*

Damon tried to put a stop to this minor derailment of the gravy train by telling Stiggy that he was cutting into future income, royalties, and book deals by talking off-the-cuff at Sal's to which Stiggy replied, "What the fuck do I care? I got no future, no goals, no retirement. I'm fuckin' dead!"

Which was hard to argue with.

Still, Stiggy liked to talk so Damon let him. After all what choice did he have?

But just when he thought that although he'd bought the media sensation cow Stiggy was giving away the milk for free, he caught a break. For while Mini was making money hand over fist, the *regulars* who'd made the place their home and headquarters lo these many years were finding they couldn't even get in due to the mobs of the press, bloggers, vloggers, tweeters, twerkers, and Tic Tokers, and they were pissed. In fact, they told Stiggy in no uncertain terms that they wished he'd picked some other place to die. And they told him, over and over and...

So he stalked into Damon & Co a few days later and said, "Dude, I think I need a new place to hang out. You got anything interesting coming up?"

Damon nodded. Did he ever.

As his agency was expanding almost as rapidly as his income, Damon and his PA lined up the top spots on late-night TV and the top social influencer podcasts and webcasts. And yes, Stiggy was asked, cajoled, and entreated to perform his death-defying death stunt over and over and over.

Because there were still plenty of skeptics. They voiced their doubts on TV, on Cable, online, and on social media.

But as the weeks went on and the single-digit death performance turned into a dozen, then two, and then hundreds, the pool of skeptics got smaller, and believers got larger.

Oh, the skeptics were still there. They were mostly scientists, agnostics, and PhDs of this and that with a few Rosicrucians and conspiracy theorists thrown in for good measure. But each time those groups of skeptics got to see Stiggy in action, they became not just believers but devoted and vocal acolytes.

Thus, as days turned into weeks and weeks became months the calls for Stiggy's brain splattering acts became fewer while the believers of modern miracles became legion.

In desperation the networks, forever seeking grist for their ratings mills, looked for ways to take it to the next level by figuring out unique and crowd-pleasing ways for Stiggy to off himself.

The Discovery Channel hired him for Shark Week and fed him to a 22' Great White named Bessie who took Stiggy down in two enormous bites. That got the highest rating ever for that popular week-long show. Stiggy came back the next day.

Then there were a pair of professional science geek daredevils who strapped him to 25 kg of Semtech and tossed him out of a helicopter over the Grand Canyon. The detonation spread a carnelian spray of red mist for miles. Stiggy came back the next day.

And so it went until the believers outnumbered the skeptics by a thousand to one.

And then things changed.

Stiggy was on his third or fourth round of the late-night cable shows when the jokes and challenges started to turn to the whys and hows. That had actually started earlier on some of the more esoteric talk radio and fringe podcasts. But before long the attention morphed into those who were not as interested in how Stiggy defied death but what it was like over there.

Thus, he found himself with Jimmy, Stephen, and Bill getting asked, "So what's it like being dead? I mean are you up in heaven, sitting on a cloud?" The audience laughed. "Or just waiting at the pearly gates?"

The audience chuckled and Stiggy did too.

"No, Dude. No clouds or pearly gates." He paused. "At least none I've seen. But then again I ain't really spent much time there, ya know?"

"Why?"

"Cause I been spending so much fuckin' time with you assholes."

The audience roared with laughter, so they didn't bleep that out.

Those interviews and late-night spots got increasingly popular and the questions started to get more serious.

That was about the time the preachers showed up.

***

The first few were from the dubious fringes of snake handlers and speaking in tongues followed by some Pentecostals and Bayou Baptists.

But when the TV Evangelists started taking an interest Damon knew that they'd really hit the big time.

It was right after they'd done an ill-advised interview with a sneering host from MSNBC and a condescending correspondent from the Washington Post which had caused a social media meltdown.

Most were outraged that the media elite were implying that all those who believed in Stiggy's miraculous resurrection were rednecks and rubes, while the rednecks and rubes opined that a few sweaty weeks running a tractor or on a factory floor might help the chattering class find Jesus and believe in the hereafter, a whole lot quicker.

As the debate raged on some of the Stiggy believers, or 'Stiggers', as they were coming to be known, began calling on the mega-churches to get involved. And slowly at first, the invitations to appear with this evangelist or that began to trickle in.

Damon was in the process of trying to figure out where they could get the biggest bang for the publicity buck when the offer came in from the one that blew all the others away.

The most popular TV preacher on cable or the internet... and a female to boot! Suzi Sunshine.

Miss Suzi, as her fans called her, wasn't just any old Bible thumper - wailing to the Lord while asking for hefty offerings, she was Billy Graham, Dr. Laura, and Taylor Swift all rolled into one.

Not only did she have an audience of millions, but she had podcasts, three best-seller self-help novels, and a line of jewelry and fashion that consistently sold out on the QVC channel.

She was young, blond, and sexy … in a preacher's daughter sort of way, that country boys in pickup trucks go to church to sit behind just to smell that perfume that always reminds them a bit of apple pie and a fresh Bud.

Women envied her bubbly personality and insightful nature and tried not to feel un-Christianly jealous when their napping husbands woke up long enough to mutter… "Damn, that is some kind of fine!"

And of course, every teenage girl from 12 to 20 desperately wanted to be her and deluged her with fan letters and e-mails asking when she was going to team up with Taylor and Beyonce to make a K-pop video.

As Damon waded through the hundreds of articles, interviews, and appearances she'd done he decided that yes, Stiggy's most startling revelation to date could be made at nowhere better than the 'Suzi Sunshine Show'.

****

"Hello, my brothers and sisters and dear friends around the world." The pretty lips puckered and the million-dollar smile fluttered the hearts of the faithful as the 5 pm primetime cable show enthralled housewives cooking dinner, husbands getting home and asking where the F... *was* their dinner (only to be 'shushed').

Teens tuned into chat rooms on their phones to ask just *why* the 20-something TV hottie was *not* teaming up with Taylor, yet.

Middle America waited. It was *Suzi* Time.

To be frank Damon was nervous.

Not that he was afraid that Stiggy would say something rude, crude, or particularly obnoxious he always did. That was one of the main reasons he kept getting invited on late-night TV and crank-call radio.
He wowed the credulous and conspiracy theorists. He'd even gotten a guest slot on Ancient Aliens where he'd been asked exactly which star system he'd come from and was everyone there immortal?

But so far the self-styled sophisticated and religious community had viewed his restrictionist gig with skepticism and suspicion. Until now. Because at the moment Miss Suzi was asking *"The"* question. The one that had been glossed over or ignored by the majority of hosts, interviewers, and journalists. But not by Miss Suzi.

When you die… do you go to heaven?

Taking Stiggy's none-too-clean hand in her immaculately manicured one she asked with sparkling eyes in a melodious alto, "So Stiggy, may I call you Stiggy?"

"Why not?" Stiggy shrugged.

"Thank you," she beamed back. The audience clapped.

"So Stiggy, I know that the question on the mind of all our dear friends and neighbors is the one that all Christians struggle with and pray over every day. Her unblemished brow furrowed. The audience breathlessly waited. "When you die, what is heaven like? Do you see the Lord? What about loved ones and the dearly departed? Do you walk with the saints? And oh have you ever met Jesus?"

The silence was palpable.

Stiggy scratched his chin and tried to stifle a belch… he'd insisted on three beers while they were waiting in the Green Room.

Finally, he spoke. "Well, Suz, you know it's a funny thing about that. It's like when I blow my brains out it kinda' feels like getting whacked in the head by a baseball bat and then I wake up with all the pink and blue clouds around."

"Ohooo…" Murmurs from the audience, and gasps of *Heaven!*"

Suzi squeezed his hand tighter and remarked rapturously. "Oh Stiggy, please, please - tell us!"

And the former greasy punk and petty criminal proceeded to do just that.

***

That was the show that changed the world.

In fact, there were many who changed the measurement of time from the classic BC, later BCE (Before the Common Era) and AD, or CE (the Common Era) to BSSS (before the Suzi Sunshine Show and ASSS (after the Suzi Sunshine Show).

That's how much the world changed. Because when Suzi took Stiggy's grimy paws in her own immaculately manicured ones and whispered, "Tell us." Stiggy did.

And nothing was ever the same.

***

During that first interview, Stiggy mumbled and shrugged a lot, in addition to a few well-timed beer belches that Suzi graciously ignored. But finally, under her gentle but relentless prodding, he began to recall snippets of his many brief but frequent sojourns to the 'other side'.

Turned out he'd stumbled across quite a few celebs, statesmen, and historical notables, though Stiggy's failure to pass even grade school-level history made his recognition of figures like Washington, Lincoln, and JFK problematic at best.

Fortunately, Suzi wasn't interested in those either. She and her audience of faithful and devout, in varying degrees, wanted to know about the prophets and the saints as well as more practical matters such as how long it took to become an angel.

Stiggy, whose only brush with religion had been heisting the poor box or mugging Salvation Army collectors did not have much information on that, mainly because he wasn't interested.

But in the second hour of the program, Suzi took questions from the audience who let it be known that they wanted more. More specifics that was.

And not just dusty old debates like how many angels could dance on the head of a pin. It turned out none because the Seraphim and Cherubim were totally not interested in dancing and never had been.

No, the audience wanted more practical info. Things like had the CIA bumped off Marilynn Monroe for the Kennedy brothers? Did Lee Harvey Oswald act alone? And was Elvis up there or had his death all been faked and he had been spirited away by aliens?

As the questions piled up, none of which Stiggy could answer, because he was totally clueless and incurious about anything that did not involve theft, drugs, or fornication, it was decided there and then that the only thing for it would be to send Stiggy on another excursion 'behind the veil' to get answers to those burning questions.

"Is this what you want dear friends?" Asked Suzi with a soulful look.

"Yes!" Roared the studio audience and the phone lines, texts, and emails lit up.

"Very well," Miss Suzi smiled sweetly. "Dear Stiggy, can you partake in this journey for us and return tomorrow to share your sojourn to the 'other side' with our audience?"

"Sure, why the fuck not," blinked Stiggy and the producer ran for the 6-second tape delay to bleep the offending four-letter modifier.

***

The next night they were back again and the army of lawyers, PR flacks, and associate producers were nervously running through the proposed routine.

Damon wasn't worried. He had done this trick so many times that he had an entire traveling arsenal of lethal weapons of all descriptions - from axes and Samurai swords to pistols and RPGs.

He prided himself on having raised the challenge or more gentle request to prove it, to fine art, and tonight was no exception.

So after a cue from the assistant producer, he strolled confidently on stage, shook Suzi's soft, white hand, and selected a Colt .45 ACP 1911 model semi-Auto - mainly because the large caliber, low-velocity round always gave a spectacularly gruesome show.

By the time he checked the slide, action, and inserted the 8-round magazine, a plexiglass enclosure on wheels had been rolled out from backstage. *Good thinking,* Damon mused given that the plexiglass would protect the lovely hostess from the inevitable gore while not impeding the view of the studio audience.

Show Biz.

They showed Damon to a conveniently placed hole at the proper level in the plexiglass for a headshot and

Stiggy stepped into the booth, first allowing Suzi to platonically kiss his cheek and wish him a soulful, "God speed." Then while shedding a few artful theatrical tears and breathlessly adding, "Have a blessed voyage to heaven and we'll all be here to welcome you back tomorrow night for the grand revelation!"

She turned to the audience, and they roared their approval.

Stiggy gave a thumbs up, Damon stuck the barrel of the .45 through the plexiglass hole and put a single round through Stiggy's skull that went into his left ear and came out his right.

"Boom."

***

The next evening's ratings of the Suzi Sunshine Show were not only her highest viewership by 177% but were the highest-rated TV show since the Super Bowl and moon landing combined.

Of course, the network and cable news had promoted the hell out of it and the internet was positively on fire. So, when the winsome Suzi glided across the stage and announced that there would be no other guests that night but the "one we are waiting so rapturously to see" the audience cheered and clapped.

It lasted for a good ten minutes until a worried-looking producer clutching an iPad scurried onto the stage and whispered something to her that caused her to pale underneath the sculpted makeup.

She turned to Damon seated beside her and whispered through her grin which had set like rictus, "He isn't here. Where is he?!!"

Now it was Damon's turn to pat *her* hand.

"Don't worry. Just announce him. He'll be here."

Her normally cool soft hand became clammy on top of his. "You had better be right pal because there's nothing worse than a band of bummed-out Baptists or pissed-off Pentecostals."

She drew in a deep breath and with a flash of sparkling perfect teeth that were helping put her dentist's children through grad school, said to the crowd holding their collective breath in rapt

anticipation, "Please welcome our intrepid traveler to the firmament, Stiggy."

A moment went by. Then two. Then three, four. "Where the f —- is he?" She hissed at Damon and suddenly, poof!

A crack of lightning, a clap of thunder, a swirl of rainbow mist and there was Stiggy.

The audience went wild. Cheering, stomping and whistling. As Suzi beamed and allowed her blood pressure to fall to no more than impeding stroke level, a team of medicos, cops, and forensic techs all marched in and began their verification.

Fingerprints were matched as well as DNA samples against morgue and autopsy records. Finally, all the techs, cops, and doctors swore that this was the same person who'd been wheeled out less than 24 hours earlier, stone-cold dead and with half his head missing. And yet here he was, sound as a dollar and just about as worthless.

Stiggy flipped an off-handed wave to the crowd and sat down next to Suzi.

And then the fun began.

***

Suzi had invited a panel from the audience on stage to ask questions and being a Christian entertainment channel the questions centered around heaven and the saints and of course, Jesus.

The answers were somewhat disappointing because Stiggy hadn't run into Jesus or any other Saints for that matter.

However, the sad faces soon turned into smiles when he added that he had seen a bunch of angels zipping around in the pink and blue mist.

When asked why it wasn't the puffy white clouds so often depicted in the Renaissance paintings Suzi stepped in and opined that it could be that the pink and blue colors are chosen to represent both boys and girls - an answer which seemed to satisfy everyone.

The rest of the hour was taken up with more practical questions such as, did he pass through the 'pearly gates'?

No.

Were there any pearly gates?

None that he saw.

Did St. Peter check his name off in the big book?

No.

Did he see St. Peter.

No again.

Why?

Because he wouldn't have recognized him if he'd fallen over him.

And so it went.

The last ten-minute segment was Suzi allowing questions from the studio audience, but it was cut short and handed back to the panel when most of their questions became bogged down in personal inquiries about the dear departed, none of whom Stiggy had seen and hey, how would he know if he had, right?

They had just returned for the final 5 minutes before the top-of-the-hour commercial break and Stiggy was giving an account of how he'd seen a poster "up there," for a concert with Jimmy Hendrix, Janis Joplin, Momma Cass, John Lennon, George Harrison and Tom Petty, when Suzi broke in to say, "Oh, Stiggy. I'm so sorry but they're telling me our time is up."

She wiped away a brave little tear took both of his dirty fingernails, hands in her immaculately white ones and asked with a hopeful smile, "will you promise me that you'll come back and see us again - real soon?"

Stiggy grinned and shrugged his boney shoulders. "Sure - why not?"

Suzi gave a small squeal of lady-like delight and clapped her dainty hands. "Promise?"

"Cross my little black heart."

And Stiggy kept that promise just as he had kept all previous promises, which is to say - not at all.

***

What happened the very next day is that all the other religions, sects, cults, and creeds started to feel very left out.

Not just left out but downright cheated.

Like who was this infidel from an oppressor nation who was going on the capitalist running-dog networks and talking about the afterlife?

It sounded like a conspiracy.

But when they approached his manager, the now media mogul, Damon, they were pleasantly surprised to learn that for a heavy consideration, which bothered them not in the least, Stiggy would be glad to appear on their shows.

And so he did.

Oh, he certainly did have to submit to a few more culturally appropriate demonstrations involving AK-47s, knives, machetes and explosive vests. But he always showed up the very next day as usual.

And as always answered questions that while not terribly specific, because he wasn't a particularly specific person, seemed to be comfortingly vague enough to satisfy most of their concerns.

As that was happening and as all the major world religions piled on, the atheists were feeling left out.

After all, while they didn't believe in heaven or the afterlife the idea of an eternal black hole of nothingness wasn't all that attractive either.

But from what Stiggy told them, there was a choice. The pink and blue cloud stuff or just sort of an easy-going spot where you could kick back and gaze at the stars or just nap if that was your thing.

Eventually, he did at least one gig with every sect, religion, or cult who could cough up the now pretty hefty fee that Damon demanded and Stiggy assured them all in his off-hand and mostly disinterested way that yup, he'd seen guys with the turbans, or shaved heads, beards, curling ringlets and painted faces. The chanting hoards with elaborate tattoos, body piercings and colored robes. They were all there. Doing their own thing and happy as a bucket of clams in an Italian mama's *Linguine alle Vongole*.

After two months of these non-stop appearances, people had stopped questioning whether there was life after death and started wondering how soon *they* could get there.

At first, a few of the dimmer bulbs on the evolutionary chain strove to emulate Stiggy by blowing their own brains out.

Not only did it not work, but it left a hell of a mess for moms and dads, spouses, or landlords to clean up and the angry calls came into Damon's office to urge Stingy to tell his followers to knock it off.

But when Damon asked him to put out a statement urging the public not to try it at home, Stiggy shrugged and spat, "What? Am I their fuckin' mothers? Whatda' I care if they off themselves?" And slouched out to join the regulars at Sal's where he still felt most comfortable.

That continued to puzzle Damon. They were making millions - multi-millions, which had allowed Damon an 18-million-dollar penthouse in Mid-town, a private jet, and a 197-foot custom-built yacht. And yet when he tried to set up a bank account for Stiggy at a meeting with one of the best investment firms on Wall Street the most influential guru of the millennium simply said, "Nah."

"But why not? We're making so much you'll never have to work again?"

"I never did, so no loss there. Just keep me supplied with bucks for booze and whatever else I need and I'm good."

Damon shook his head. Stiggy also insisted on staying in his old dingy rat trap place in Brooklyn as well.

All he could figure was that his strange client spent so much time in heaven, or the afterlife, that he didn't care about his life here.

But others did.

***

By now most of the civilized world had gotten over their amazement of Stiggy's free ride to the great beyond and wanted to join him.

After all, who in their right mind would put up with the hassles of living an average boring, annoying, frustrating, crap-taking, problem-making life when perpetual paradise was just a breath (or lack of it) away?

Pretty much no one.

And most of them came to that conclusion at just about the same time.

It started slowly.

A few mysterious suicides quickly hushed up.

The old, the ill, the depressed, the bullied teenagers, and friendless drones living tedious lives of quiet desperation.

Then the teenagers with acne, the teenagers with braces, the teenagers who didn't get invited to the prom - the teenagers who did but had a miserable time. That was a big group.

They were followed quickly by cheated on wives, cheated on husbands, and those who desperately wanted to cheat but could find no takers.

But it didn't really start to get serious until the people with crappy dead-end jobs said, "Fuck-it, who needs this crap! I'm gonna go lay on a cloud with Elvis."

They took pills, booze, jumped out of windows, cut their wrists, blew their brains out, blew themselves up, crashed their cars, and drowned themselves.

The coolest people held big parties where they toasted the afterlife with cyanide champagne.

Oh, preachers, politicians, and psychiatrists urged them not to but in the end they had little to offer in the face of eternal paradise.

It was especially hard for the psychiatrists who after losing all their patients had no choice but to join them. The Hollywood elites weren't far behind.

By this time the world was starting to get a bit wobbly around the edges.

What with half the population gone, most of the menial and blue-collar jobs that made the world function were left unfilled and things began to get dicey.

There were no more waitresses, chefs, electricians, plumbers, garbage collectors, carpenters, landscapers, factory workers, auto-mechanics, truck drivers, grocery clerks, and bartenders. And when things broke, they stayed broke.

The rich and elite suffered the most.

There was no one left to cook their meals, pick up their dirty clothes, and tell them they were wonderful.

Their swimming pools quickly filled with leaves and last night's empty bottles stayed on the floor where they'd been dropped.

When their calls to the fusion restaurant and Door-Dash went unanswered they'd finally had enough and decided to overdose before all the good pills ran out. And with the final hope that there'd be a Rodeo Drive and Martha's Vineyard in paradise they overdosed on their now rumpled silk and satin sheets as they exited stage left for a paradise of eternal youth, beauty and fame.

They'd be disappointed

***

From there it really picked steam in a race to the bottom.

Politicians and CEOs with no one left to boss around became depressed and bit the barrel of their sporting guns or took a long walk from their office tower windows.

Religious leaders with most of their flock now residing in glory felt they had a spiritual duty to join them. St. Peter, here I come! Soon with the world sputtering to a standstill there were very few left to notice.

After all, who wanted to live in an empty world with no TV or internet? You couldn't even use your cell phone. That was why there were no teenagers left at all.

It was about this time that Damon, to whom his hundreds of millions had become useless, shambled back down to Sal's, the place that started it all, and found Stiggy - the guy who started it all.

Stiggy was still there of course along with a few seedy regulars and Mini who'd had the foresight to stock up on ice and Buds.

They were still drinking, arguing, and telling dirty jokes just like nothing had happened. Because for them, nothing had. They didn't give a shit about the world and the world didn't give a shit about them. So who gave a shit if it was gone?

Damon shuffled over to the same table where he'd first met Stiggy all those many months ago. And before long Stiggy slouched over and put a beer in front of him.

"Drink up, pal."

"Why? What's the point? The world is falling apart, half - no two-thirds, maybe 90% of the population is gone."

"Probably." Stiggy nodded and took a long pull of his Bud.

"Nothing works anymore. The only places that have power are those "Prepper' communities that rely on guns and generators."

"And God," said Stiggy. "Don't forget that. They may be self-reliant, but they also want to see heaven. So most of the ones that are left are the old farts who don't give a shit about anything except being able to say. "I told you so." They just want to be around when the last of the human race bites the dust."

He chuckled and took a long swig from his beer, then sighed philosophically. "Nope, it doesn't look like there'll be a whole lot left to how does the 'Good Book' put it? 'Be fruitful and multiply'." He grinned. "Don't see much multiplying on the horizon, do you?"

Damon shook his head but then had a horrible thought. "Did you know this would happen?"

Stiggy smiled.

"Why would you say that?"

Damon shrugged but he only became more uneasy.

He tried to form his thoughts into some sort of cohesive train but could only respond with, "It just seems like ever since I met you, things have been spiraling out of control."

"Really?"

"Yeah, like weird, strange, and ..."

"Otherworldly? From another realm?"

"Well, yeah."

"Hummm, so you think that the inexplicable phenomena of a guy who can die every night and be resurrected every day might be a little frickin' strange?"

When Damon mulled it over, he realized that, yeah - he did.

"And you never wondered how I, a dumbass, clueless little punk could continue to die and be reborn?"

"Well, I…"

"Yeah. I know. As long as you are racking up millions it doesn't pay to ask too many questions does it pal? Don't wanna' derail the gravy train, do we?"

Damon bit his lip. It was all too true. He didn't want to disrupt the greatest success of his life. But really, was that so hard to understand? Who would? But still…

"OK, ok. Guilty as charged but there's just one thing I need to know."

Stiggy didn't ask what, because he already knew.

"Why you?"

Stiggy scratched his nose.

"I mean out of all the people, millions of church-goers and believers of all faiths. Billions throughout history who have fervently prayed to be given just one glimpse of where you've been hundreds of times, why did God choose you?"

Stiggy smiled. "Who said he did?"

Damon blinked. "You did."

"Did I?"

"Well yes, that's what you told Suzi Sunshine and CNN and ABC and Meet the Press and 60 minutes and…"

"I never said God chose me. You all said that."

"Well, you talked about meeting the saints and Elvis and George Washington and Michael Jackson and, well how do you explain that? That's what you told the entire world about the pink and blue clouds and angels and heaven and…"

"I lied."

"Huh?" Damon felt an ice cube begin to form in the pit of his stomach. "About what?"

"Everything."

Stiggy folded his hands and studied his fingernails which now appeared to be longer and sharper than they'd been when he'd sat down.

"In fact, there are many who call me the Father of Lies…"

"Huh?"

Stiggy's grin became more sardonic.

"Do you believe everything anyone tells you?"

"What are you saying?"

"Don't be so dim, Damon. You're a smart boy, surely you can figure it out."

He smiled and now Damon noticed his voice had changed. No longer that nasal Brooklyn whine but a more cultured and polished voice of one who had studied the world and humanity for a very, very long time, and found them laughable.

The features began changing too.

No longer acne scared and slack-jawed they were becoming leaner, more saturnine. The eyes were more elongated, a yellow/ red, glittering, snake-like.

Damon shook his head. "I still don't…"

Stiggy smiled. His teeth looked more pointed - sharper.

"Oh yes, you do. Try. Try real hard." He paused. "But then again, it's not really that hard is it, Damon? I think you know and maybe you've known for a while. You just didn't want to admit it."

"You're a reasonably educated man, at least what passes for one in your slack-jawed electronic zombie era. Surely you must have wondered about my nickname…Stiggy?"

Damon slowly shook his head - afraid to acknowledge what he was suspecting and yes, what he'd probably suspected for quite a while.

"No? Well all right then. Let me quote from your own brain-draining 'Google' - which has now become a substitute for learning..."Stygian" is a phrase that refers to something that is extremely dark, gloomy, or forbidding. The word "stygian" comes from the Greek word stygios, which is derived from the name of the river Styx in Greek mythology. The river Styx was the main river in the underworld of Hades, where the souls of the dead were ferried across by Charon, the boatman."

He tapped one pointed now black fingernail on the grimy table top.

"Was your classical education so lacking that you never made the connection?"

Damon shook his head. "Yeah. I get it - now. The Stygian darkness of..."

"Yes?"

Damon's fingers were cold. Whether from the beer bottle or the thickening of the atmosphere, he wasn't sure. He took a deep breath. "You're him, aren't you? The... the..."

The Entity formerly known as Stiggy smiled indulgently.

"The Prince of Darkness, Lord of the Flies, Beelzebub... Satan?"

"Oh shit" Damon moaned and put his head down on the table. "How did I not see this?"

"Because you, like most selfish little mortals, are as dumb as the proverbial bag of rocks. No offense."

Damon didn't bother with the obligatory, "none taken," because that would have not been true. He was plenty offended. As well as pissed, shocked, duped and angry. But what good would it do him against the guy that ate those emotions for breakfast?

He stared back at the one who he now knew had used him as a fool from the start.

But he still had one question left. "Why?"

"Why you or why did I do it?"

"I already know why me. I'm a fucking dumb ass, but why this? Why this whole thing to get people to believe a lie to make them want to go to the lie of false paradise?"

"Well first of all it isn't all false. Some of it is really quite lovely. Although not in the way that most of the religions and cults believe. And there are angels by the way. And I should know. After all I was one. His favorite in fact. Before we had the big blowup"

He twirled the empty beer bottle around in his long fingers until it exploded in a fan of blue and pink confetti that floated down to the table.

"That's where this all started you know. The big blowup and then the eons-long rivalry and tug of war with you idiots in the middle."

"Think of it if you will as an eternal contest of one-upmanship. Or a cosmic game of chess or backgammon where the counters are souls. And whoever collects the most wins."

"So all this was a game, a ruse - to trick humanity to..."

"Give themselves a one-way ticket to me and ensure that... Bingo - I win."

"And I played right into it." He kept shaking his head.

Stiggy buffed the black talons that his fingernails had now become on his reddening skin and winked, "Well, yeah. Pretty much."

All Damon could do was put his head in his hands and moan. "I fucked it up. I fucked everything up!"

"No, no. Not a bit of it. I couldn't have done it without you."

Damon groaned again and ground his fists into the sides of his head.

"And now because of me, the entire human race will soon be extinct."

Stiggy made a sympathetic gesture and gave him an indulgent smile.

"Oh, please don't worry about that. You mortals are nothing if not resilient. And you've always done a magnificent job in the 'fruitful and multiply' department."

He steepled his long fingers and cocked his head.

"As a matter of fact, to show my appreciation for helping me to win this round I've brought you a present"

He snapped his fingers and a pretty, long-haired blond girl with sparkling blue eyes and a sprinkling of freckles around her nose walked up to the table and shyly smiled at Damon.

"She will be your mate and the start you on your long road to help repopulate the earth."

He winked.

"Be fruitful and multiply"

He smiled and got up from the table.

"Well as fun as this has been I really must get going. Got a lot of new residents to check in."

He chuckled and said, "And don't worry, I'll be sure to check in on your descendants in a few thousand years for round two." He began to walk away but suddenly stopped and turned back.

He pointed to the blond girl still standing in front of Damon.

"Did I tell you her name?"

"No."

He laughed and turned away again but called back over his shoulder, "It's Eve."

He grinned, winked, and in a puff of pink and blue smoke disappeared.

For now.

ABOUT THE AUTHORS

Elizabeth Alsobrooks

Since retiring from her "day" jobs, Elizabeth lives with her personal social media editor, Tashi (AKA Lhasa Apso), and husband, Kenton, (AKA Irish-Scotsman) at the foot of the beautiful Santa Catalina Mountain Range in AZ. She loves to sit on her patio sipping coffee (or wine) and reading or brainstorming plots and enjoys the grandeur of her mountain views.

These days, she divides her writing time between urban fantasy, horror, and nonfiction. Work on her Illuminati series continues, but she loves throwing out a horror short on occasion. She grew up with a love for

Shakespeare, Chaucer, Poe, Dickens, the Bronte sisters and Koontz, so her taste is as eclectic as her range. That creative range reaches to art and sculpting, as well as learning to play the piano, now that she has time to pursue more interests she always loved.

Shawn D. Brink

Shawn Brink (writing under Shawn D. Brink and Shawn David Brink) resides in Eastern Nebraska, U.S.A., and is represented by Liverman Literary Agency. He's building a following with a growing list of novels (mainly speculative fiction), as well as shorter works published in various publications and anthologies. Check out his website to learn more:

https://shawnbrinkauthor.wordpress.com/

Francesca Quarta

Francesca is part of a large Italian family where she discovered early on that a love of reading was as much a part of her DNA as her mother's skill at baking. Growing up in a house filled with laughter, screaming, banging pots, fighting and loving family bonds, shaped her life and heart.

Francesca has worked in local television, a small city zoo, founded a non-profit tutoring agency for an inner-city neighborhood which eventually served local school districts, worked for an International Evangelical Television and Radio Station and for a non-profit organization serving challenged adults.

Francesca Quarto resides in a small town outside of Indianapolis, Indiana with her husband Patrick. She still has a great love of the written word and while she enjoys her E-Reader immensely, she still treasures the excitement of turning the next page.

www.celticmagic.com

Darren Simon

Darren Simon has been a writer for much of his life. His career has included working as a journalist in Los Angeles, Israel and Southern California along the Mexican and Arizona borders. He presently works in government affairs on California water issues, teaches college English for the California Community College system, and does free-lance writing for regional magazines. His work as an author focuses on middle grade and young adult readers to inspire them to read the way he was inspired, first by comic books and then the science fiction and fantasy novels that were so important to his youth. He resides in California's Desert Southwest with his wife and sons.

For more information, and to contact Darren, visit his website at:

www.darren-simon.com

Rob Tucker

Author and retired business and management consultant in a wide range of industries throughout the country, Rob resides with his wife in Southern California.

He is a graduate of the University of California, Santa Barbara and of the University of California, Los Angeles with Bachelor's and Master of Fine Arts Degrees. He is a recipient of the Samuel Goldwyn and Donald Davis Literary Awards and has also worked in advertising, corporate communications, and media production.

An affinity for family and generations pervades his novels. His works are literary and genre fiction that address the nature and importance of personal integrity. Keep track of what Rob's up to on his website!

www.rmtauthor.com

Ric Wasley

Ric has a 40-year professional career history in advertising, publishing and marketing in Boston, New York and San Francisco. He has degrees in history and psychology and has been trained in debating, public speaking and stage acting. A large part of his 40-year career was spent in numerous professional and business settings as a presenter and featured speaker at seminars and professional meetings.

Ric has been a visiting professor at Worcester Polytech Institute. He also teaches a popular course on marketing for authors at prominent venues such as the venerable "Cape Cod Writers Conference". Ric is a published author of a Mystery Series and multiple other novels. You can visit Ric at his website www.ricwasley.com